Cut
here!

We decorated this WHOLE book with our art. Now it's YOUR turn! Decorate this mini poster, then cut it out and hang it up in your locker!

Besties

A special family member appreciates you.

It's time to nominate yourself for Student Council.

YOU FOR
class president

You and your BFF will go on a fun adventure!

Look in the mirror and shout, "You're awesome!"

World

Dreams
zzz

Study hard for your next
test. It will pay off
big-time!

It's time to drop a subtle
hint to your crush.

Make a point to learn
something new
every day!

You'll get noticed at the
school dance for
being you!

Family

Cut here

Take On the World

(or at Least Master Your Middle School Years!)

JOHN QUINCY ADAMS

How cool would it be to have a cheat sheet for middle school? Picture a teacher's edition for life, with all the answers to every question you have . . . especially the ones created to annoy and embarrass you.

Now imagine something even better: instructions written for you by your new best friends, Riley (that's me!) and Maya ('sup, girl?).

How crazy-good would that be?

Well, welcome to OUR WORLD, friend, because what you now hold in your hands is a book of answers to life's most important questions . . . or at least what we've discovered so far! We admit, we still have a lot to learn, but we want to share what we've been through to date. 'Cause nothing would make us happier than if our tips and tricks helped you OWN middle school!

BooK OF ANSWers

3

How This Guide Happened

If you're anything like us, *and we really hope you are!* at this point you're saying to yourself, "Self, why would two smart, fashionable, and fun girls waste their time teaching me how to master middle school? Sure, I'm cool, friendly, and funny, but they don't know me. So what's the deal?"

Two things:

1. Good questions! We'd be wondering the same things ourselves.

2. Fortunately, your spirit guides have figured something out: Middle school is like a maze. It's hard to navigate. It's confusing. And the people can be animals.

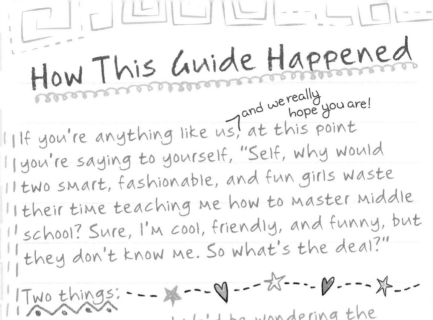

← Animal

You see, through our own experiences so far, we've become convinced that middle school was actually created by a crazy game designer who's trying to mess with your head. However, we've also discovered that if you have a friend *or, better yet, two friends!* who can put you on the right path and cheer you on as you go, middle school will start feeling less like a maze and more like amaaaaze.

↖ I see what you did there!

World, Meet Riley and Maya

Though we're, like, 99.9 percent sure you know who we are, since it kind of feels like we're besties already, for that 0.1 percent of you who'd like a little more info, allow us to introduce ourselves.

I'm Riley!

Which must make me Maya.

Got it? Good. Moving on!

Okay, okay. We'll give you a little more, but since we don't love talking about ourselves, we'll tell you about each other, and then each of us will take a crack at writing the different parts of this book.

Who Is Riley Matthews?

by Maya Hart

Aside from being my BFF, I'd describe Riley as hilarious, bubbly, kind, smart, quirky, outgoing, and at times awkward but always awesome. (Bizarrely, she loves doing homework, which makes me wonder if she's part alien. But even if she were, that'd be okay. I'd love her all the more for the antennae she'd try to camouflage with sunglasses on the top of her head.) Every now and again Riley needs some help getting a clue. But that's okay, because that's what I'm here for. This girl is the kind of person who's just so ridiculously nice and perpetually happy, you can't help but love her.

Who Is Maya Hart?

by Riley Matthews

Maya is the coolest, funnest, most confident girl in the world, and I'm proud to call her my best friend. She's witty, loyal, and always has an answer for everything, including why she never finishes her homework. (Bizarrely, she hates homework, which makes me wonder what planet she's from. But even if she were from a galaxy far, far away, I'd still adore her . . . and it would help explain a lot!) Maya fights for what she believes in, and despite her troublemaker image, Maya Hart's heart is always in the right place!

The Importance of POSITIVITY

I think happy thoughts. I believe good things will happen. I smile All. The. Time. In case you're wondering, yes, my cheeks ARE killing me—but I'm okay with that because, as Maya often tells me, I'm like a real-life happy-face emoji.

She really is!

I admit it: my name is Riley Matthews, and I'm a positivity junkie.

Why do I have such an optimistic point of view? Because my dad taught me a cool little saying, which I will happily share with you. But get ready, because it's a mind-blower:

I love hugs!

"If you can see it, you can be it."

=Mind. Blown.=

Now you may be thinking, "Huh? What?"

What it means is that if I say to myself, "Riley, you are going to have a great day today," I can make it happen, because I can envision it taking place. Being positive about things pumps me up, and once I'm in a great frame of mind, nothing can stop me.

I think the energy we give off is like a boomerang or a magnet. If you put good and happy thoughts out into the universe, you're going to attract the same kind of encouragement from others. When you're negative, dark clouds roll right back at you. Scowl at someone or criticize them and they're probably going to do the same. But if you give a smile and a compliment, that's usually what you will get in return. Who doesn't like a nice, friendly compliment? No one, that's who!

So when in doubt, smile. Believe that things are going to go well, and know that since you only live once you should be as positive about your middle school experience as you can be!

Okay, okay, it's my turn now.

Keepin' It Real

Okay, so now that you've taken a ride on that rainbow slide with Riley and have landed safely in Happyland, it's time for me to provide a reality check. Don't get me wrong—I think what Riley just said is right. And it's great advice. But in my experience, it's much harder some days than others to smile wide for the camera and convince yourself that people will assume the zit on your nose is a mark of royalty.

Thanks, Maya!

Sometimes it seems easier to lie about who you are, what you think, and what you believe in. It may seem like going with the flow—someone else's flow—is better than listening to the voice in your own head. But acting like someone you aren't, pretending you're super tough or that you don't care about what's going on around you, is just lame. #MadLame #dontmakemeturnthiscararoundlame

When you try to act like someone you're not, you're just being a poser—and who likes a poser? No one but other posers, that's who. And they're just super-duper-DUPER lame. #amiright?!

It took me a while to figure this out, but eventually I realized that the reason people like me in the first place is because of my ME-ness. I bet you'll find the same thing—that people love you for your YOU-niqueness. So do yourself and all your fans a favor and just keep being you—even when it's hard, okay? Because you're the person people want to know. (And I'm not just saying that because you're the one holding the answers to life's middle school mysteries in your hand!)

Well put, Maya!

11

Top Secret

These "top secret" pages are for your eyes only. Don't worry—not even Riley and I will read these pages. So keep it real, even if you think what you're writing sounds silly or uncool. Embrace your top-secret thoughts!

What are your strengths?

What are you afraid of?

Boo

What makes you happy?

What makes you sad or mad?

Now that you know where we stand, here's what we're going to be chatting about in the rest of this kick-butt book.

It's a little thing we like to call ○ ○ ○

Drumroll, please!

I LOVE a good drumroll!

Who doesn't?!

The Table of Contents

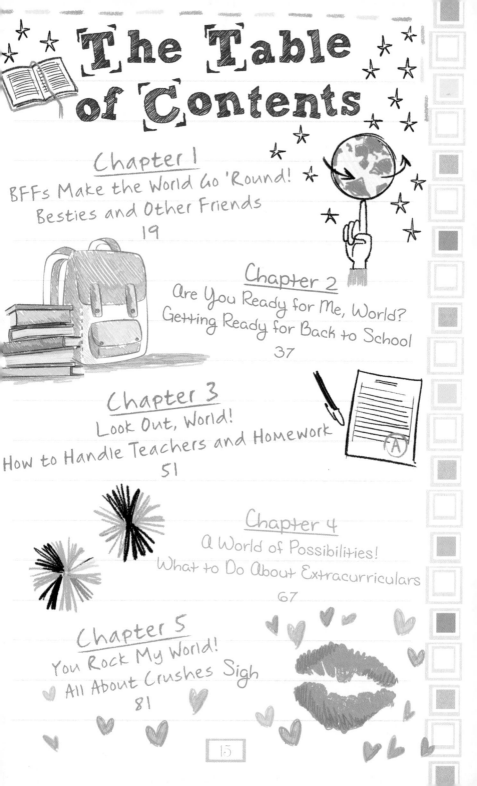

After we sat down and wrote out the table of contents, we realized that because we still don't know all the answers ourselves, it might be good to get the opinions of people who've been through this whole wild ride (a.k.a. old people) a.k.a. Riley's parents, Cory and Topanga. We have to admit, they've given both of us good advice in the past, so we hope they'll steer you right, too!

Words of Encouragement from Cory and Topanga

Well, hello there! Thanks for letting us crash your party. We promise we'll make ourselves scarce soon so you can get back to the girls. They're the real experts here. We just wanted to say that as long-ago middle schoolers ourselves, and as parents to a present-day tween, we know that a lot of the new experiences you're having now or will have in the future could be hard or confusing or frustrating . . . and probably some combination of all three! So here's what we've learned.

Having a good attitude and keeping an open mind are the two keys to success (not only in middle school but also in life). And we're confident you're going to be successful, because just look at you— you're a butterfly about to take flight!

The good-attitude thing just makes good sense, doesn't it? When you're happy and believe that anything's possible, you exude a special glow. Everyone wants to get closer to check out your sparkle.

But why is keeping an open mind so crucial? Tell us, honey. Well, it turns out when you let yourself be open to new experiences and ideas, you grow. There are more than seven billion people on planet Earth, and if you allow the possibility that they, too, have cool ideas, beliefs, and ways of dealing with things, you can learn a lot. You might even fall in love with that new thing (or person!), but let's not get ahead of ourselves here. . . .

For now we'll just leave you to your reading and wish you luck in the journey ahead. It's going to be a great trip and a heckuva ride. But we know you're going to arrive at the other end smarter, more confident, and ready to take on whatever adventure comes next! Now back to the girls.

Chapter 1

BFFs Make the World Go 'Round!

Besties and Other Friends

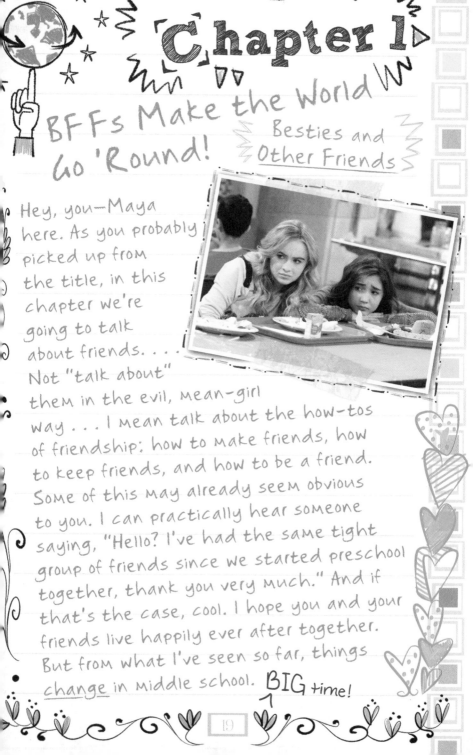

Hey, you—Maya here. As you probably picked up from the title, in this chapter we're going to talk about friends. . . . Not "talk about" them in the evil, mean-girl way . . . I mean talk about the how-tos of friendship: how to make friends, how to keep friends, and how to be a friend. Some of this may already seem obvious to you. I can practically hear someone saying, "Hello? I've had the same tight group of friends since we started preschool together, thank you very much." And if that's the case, cool. I hope you and your friends live happily ever after together. But from what I've seen so far, things <u>change</u> in middle school. BIG time!

Sometimes the people we've been friends with our whole lives suddenly decide to hang out with other people. Sometimes they start acting strangely, sitting with new friends at lunchtime and pretending all those sleepovers, epic online chats, and totally fun gossip sessions with us didn't mean anything at all to them. I have one word for that: WEAK!

So how should you handle it when you're feeling left out or like your crowd has entirely changed its tune? Well, this is what worked for me: I remembered that though 1 may feel like the loneliest number, $1 + 1 = 2$ and the

Power of 2 is LEGENDARY!

All you have to do is find ONE OTHER PERSON to hang with, and as soon as you do that, your job is done. You've reached capacity. Of course, I can't tell you if this person is destined to be your new bestie or just a friend to trade music with. Only time can tell. But from what I've seen, making and keeping friends is like planting flowers in a garden, and I'll talk about that a little more after my best friend, Riley, tells you about how to find a true BFF of your own.

Finding Your BFF

I'm excited! This is something you want to put some extra good energy into, because finding a best friend is one of the most important things you'll do in your whole life. EVER.

No pressure.

You're probably wondering how it works. You're saying, "Riley, is there some sort of test I can give to people to see if they'd be a good fit for the role of best friend?" The answer to that is, "Uh, no." Maybe you're wondering if your best friend should be the person who's considered the most attractive or most popular kid. I'd say, "Maybe?" But truthfully, that sounds superficial (hate to break it to you). You can't tell from the way someone looks if that person will be a good friend or not. It's all about personalities clicking like a seat belt.

click

So what makes a good BFF?

What Makes a Good BFF?

While there isn't a test to tell if someone is BFF material, I did make a checklist. So you've been hanging out with a few people, and you really click with one of them. If they have most of the checks in my list, they have the makings for a great BFF!

BFF Checklist

- ✓ Do I like this person?
- ✓ Does this person like me?
- ✓ Do we have fun together?
- ✓ Can we talk about anything together?
- ✓ Is this person honest with me (and can I be honest back)?
- ✓ Do we trust each other?
- ✓ Do we stay in touch even when we're not in the same place?
- ✓ When we meet after some time apart, does it feel like no time has passed?
- ✓ Does it feel like we're always in the middle of a conversation?
- ✓ Do we make each other happy when we're sad?
- ✓ Do we build each other up (and not tear each other down)?
- ✓ Do we support each other's choices?
- ✓ Can I imagine the two of us hanging out when we're older?
- ✓ Can we hang out all day without getting tired of each other?
- ✓ Can we sit together in silence without feeling awkward?

Being a Good BFF Takes Work

As I've mentioned, I think Riley's the greatest, and I know how lucky I am to have her in my life. That's why I want to make sure I do everything I can to be the best friend she deserves.

And even though it felt easy and natural to become best friends with her, making sure the relationship stays forever cool is something we both work on.

Remember how I said making and keeping friends is like planting flowers in a garden? Well, imagine your best friend is your prize rosebush: you love seeing them, they make everything better, and they smell great (hopefully). But a rose is a delicate thing and needs to be cared for, or it will droop. So if you want it to stick around in your garden, you've got to shower it with love, water it, prune it, and . . . do whatever else you do to make sure a rose stays happy.

(Hey, I'm a city girl!)

Every now and again, it's nice to remind your bestie how much you appreciate them. Of course, you don't want to drown your bestie in sappy stuff, constantly telling them how much you worship the ground they walk on, because YEEEECH. But remember their birthday, and make a big deal of it. Maybe you two have a friend-iversary. If so, figure out a little something special you can do together. You also want to balance the plan-making so it doesn't always fall on one of you. Sometimes it's nice to be thought of.

Most important, we've learned that being besties is about being there for each other— knowing when to talk and when to listen. Your bestie is the one who's going to listen to all your problems and give you the best advice they know, so you also want to make sure you're listening to them when they have something to say. With a bestie, you shouldn't have to worry about what you say, but you always want to respect their ideas. No issue of your bestie's is ever too small! They have your back and you've got theirs.

Trust Is ... Kind of Important

What I discovered last year was that being able to trust that your bestie is always, **ALWAYS** on your side—through thick and thin, pimples, bad haircuts, and crazy outfits—is how you know you've got a great person in your corner.

You need to be able to trust your best friend. The time of life we're going through now is INSANELY confusing, and making mistakes is a huge part of it. You need to feel confident that your best friend isn't going to make fun of you when you trip over your own two feet, or stand you up, or spill your secrets all over social media.

And the flip side of that is that YOU need to be trustworthy. You can't let down your best friend, right? You adore them, and they're counting on you. That's exactly how it is with Maya and me. You need to be there for them, even if it means telling a white lie to protect their feelings. You also need to be honest with your bestie and not let them embarrass themselves if they're doing something totally lousy or, worse, if they're doing something dangerous. You both need to promise each other that you'll help each other make it through the jungle of middle school (and beyond), because it can be scary. Fortunately, with your bestie by your side, it can be super fun, too!

Best Friend 4EVER Quiz

1. If someone starts talking smack about your friend when your friend is not around, what do you do?

    a. Start calling the person names. (3)

    b. Tell the person you disagree and explain why. (2)

    c. Mention the thing you like least about your BFF. (1)

2. The person you've been crushing on asks your bestie out on a date instead of you! What do you say to your bestie?

    a. Tell your bestie to have fun and enjoy themselves. (3)

    b. Tell your bestie that your friendship is over if they go. (1)

    c. Tell your bestie it would mean a lot to you if they don't go. (2)

3. Your friend's favorite outfit hasn't been in style since the 1990s. What do you do?

    a. Nothing! I don't care what my bestie wears. I'm focused on what's inside. (2)

    b. I gently suggest that my bestie would look so great in the new style of the day and offer to go shopping with them. (3)

    c. I'd be real with my bestie. No need to sugarcoat the truth! (1)

4. You and your friend are going out on a Friday night. What do you wear?

    a. Whatever. I don't need to dress to impress my friend. (1)

    b. Same thing my BFF's wearing. I like to coordinate! (3)

    c. Something my bestie will think is supercool. (2)

5. You have plans to hang out with your BFF at their house, but a better option comes along. What do you do?

    a. Fake sickness and tell your BFF you don't want to infect them. (1)

    b. Tell your BFF the truth and try to snag an invitation for them, too. (2)

    c. Go to your BFF's house and don't think twice. Your BFF comes first! (3)

6. How often do you and your BFF communicate when you're not together?

    a. As much as humanly and technologically possible. (3)

    b. Not a ton. Out of sight is kind of out of mind. (1)

    c. A couple of times a day. (2)

7. What's your favorite thing about your BFF?

    a. My BFF's the most popular kid in school! (1)

    b. We can talk for hours about nothing. (3)

    c. I always learn something cool from my BFF. (2)

Now add up the numbers next to your answers.

7-13: Is this REALLY your best friend, or just someone who's playing the part for a while? Though you don't have a lot in common, remember to be good to each other and respect each other while you're hanging out.

14-18: You and your bestie are like a hand and glove; you're made for each other! Good times, bad times, and everything crazy in between, you've been through it all together, and your friendship only gets stronger with each passing year!

19-21: Talk about an intense relationship! You and your BFF share everything from brain laughs to brain waves! You're basically siblings separated at birth.

Score: _____

Make Up Your Own
Handshake of
AWESOMENESS

When we saw Lucas and Billy do their handshake, we were totally JELLY. If boys have a special handshake, girls need one, too, right? Right! Now from the outside it might look like we just spontaneously came up with all the moves because we're best friends and can read each other's minds. But it's not quite that easy. The first thing we did was brainstorm a list of possible gestures (like fist bumping, finger snapping, elbow-to-wrist sliding, foot tapping, hip shaking, butt bumping, etc., etc., etc.), then we had to decide what order it would go in, and then we practiced . . . and . . . and practiced until it looked like we'd been born doing it.

Create your own handshake of AWESOMENESS!

Signs of a Toxic BFF

If they have these traits . . . run!

1. Doesn't support you

2. Constantly criticizes you

3. Tries to one-up you

4. Can't be relied on

5. Only there when they need something

6. Acts jealous of you

7. Makes you feel guilty

8. Gets you in trouble

9. Wants you to try dangerous things

10. Takes credit for all your stuff

11. Acts super negative

12. Manipulates you

13. Acts self-centered

14. Makes immoral choices

15. Acts insincere

16. Isn't considerate

Making Additional Friends Can Be Fun, Too!

You know that moment when you find EXACTLY the right pair of jeans? You slip them on, zip 'em up, slide the button into its slot, and you're like, "Ahhhhh." They feel SOOOO good. You s l o w l y open the dressing-room door and drift to the full-length mirror at the other end of the fitting room. These magical jeans not only fit like a dream, but they look SLAMMIN' on you, too. Well, guess what?

Making FRIENDS can give you exactly the same feeling. Friends are a lot like jeans—when you find the right ones, there's no better feeling. Now this is not to say that every friend (or every pair of pants) is going to be the right fit. Sometimes they just don't work no matter how hard you try. Maybe they make you feel uncomfortable in some way. Maybe they're just not for you. That's totally okay. I've found that "trying things on for size" can be interesting and has introduced me to lots of new stuff. So even if something (or someone) seems too wild or conservative for your taste, you never know how you'll feel until you give it (or them) a try.

How to Handle Bullies

Okay, I'm going to assume you now know all we can teach you about finding and being a good friend. So it's time to talk about the opposite—being bullied and/or being a bully.

Bullies have been around since the dawn of time. But in the days of the dinosaurs, at least you could see them coming, 'cause they were giant, ugly beasts hunting for their next innocent victim.

Today, bullies can be even worse.

From what I've experienced, they walk around school undercover. One minute, they seem perfectly normal and friendly; the next, they're lashing out at you and making you feel as small as a mouse.

So what should you do if you're the target of one of these beasts? Well, from what I've seen, there are a lot of different kinds of bullying. That's why, in my humble opinion, I don't think anyone can say, "Just do this one thing!" and it'll work every time. But talking about it with someone you trust is usually a really great place to start. You're not being a tattletale or uncool if you tell another person. Maya and I actually have a word for that. We call it "wise."

You've probably heard someone say, "It gets better," and though it may seem hard to believe, I swear it's true: the bullying will stop eventually, and life will get easier. I know, I know. . . . I bet you're thinking, "Great, Riley, but what does that do for me NOW? And how am I supposed to handle the bullying that starts as soon as I get to school in the morning?"

You have a totally fair point.

That's why I have a few ideas you can try right away:

- Tell the bully to stop. It might give the bully something to think about if you tell them to knock it off and throw a little shame in their game. You could say something like: "Why are you acting this way? You don't even know me."

- If you think someone might actually hurt you physically, find a safe place—a classroom with a teacher, a crowd where you have an ally, a place where adults are present— and stay there until the threat is gone.

- If someone's bullying you online, don't react or reply. Why? Because it NEVER works. Responding usually only makes the person more aggressive. So just save the message as a screenshot or in a folder in your e-mail. It could come in handy as evidence if the situation escalates.

- Block the e-mail addresses and phone numbers of people sending you hateful messages. No need for you to see that kind of negativity.

Vent. It's important you get your feelings out and not hold them inside. Find someone you trust who is a good listener, and talk it out. It doesn't have to be a parent. It can be a teacher you really like, a counselor, or someone you trust and think is smart. You don't have to face this alone.

Journal. Write down your feelings. Don't hold them in!

Make a list. If you're being bullied and people are constantly saying mean things, you can get to a point where you start believing those mean things, even though they're not true. Don't fall into that trap! Write a list of all the positive qualities you have, and read through it daily. Add new qualities as they come to mind. Remind yourself each and every day how wonderful you are, and don't let anyone take away the amazing traits that make you, you. If someone other than you is being bullied, go out of your way to give them a compliment and remind them how wonderful they are. Also, feel free to lend them this great book.

Like I said before, I haven't seen or heard of a guaranteed way to stop a bully from trying to make your life miserable. But talking about the problem with someone else or writing about it is super helpful. Don't let a bully bring you down. You're too wonderful to let someone else crush that great spirit of yours!

There's a light inside of you that shines. Don't let anyone stifle it.

A

The Bullyer Gabby in 2nd grad.

me

Write a list of all the positive qualities you like about yourself. Try to fill up the whole page.

PS: You rock!

Friendship Tips

My two favorite girls did a great job explaining the ins and outs of friendship in this chapter, so I don't have much more to add. But as someone who's kept great friends from the time she was your age, what's meant the most to me is knowing that my friends always want the best for me. Sometimes it's a friend's job to give you constructive criticism. You want to know if you're doing something wrong or hurtful or stupid, and trust me, it's best to hear about this from our friends instead of our enemies. I know hearing criticism is never easy. That's why it's incredibly important to know that your friend is telling you these things only because he or she loves you and wants you to be the best you that you can be.

This is the kind of thing that requires a great deal of trust from you both—and you need to promise to help each other out when the need arises. But once you're sure your friend has nothing but good intentions, it's easier to make the changes you need to make. And remember, you can't get angry at your friend for telling you the truth, tough as it may be—especially if you're asking for it. You just need to remind yourself that this person loves you and is looking out for you.

Topanga

Chapter 2

Are You Ready for Me, World?

Getting Ready for Back to School

JOHN QUINCY ADAMS

> For me, the most exciting time of
> the year—aside from my birthday
> (because duh!)—is the week
> before school starts. By that
> point I'm completely chilled out
> from my great summer vacation. I've
> paged through every one of the coolest fashion
> magazines, seen all the hottest blockbuster
> movies and TV shows, downloaded hit songs,
> customized my phone, and thrown my little
> brother, Auggie, out of my room more times
> than I can count.

In the week before school begins, thoughts dance through my head at about a million miles an hour. That's because, for me, the start of each school year feels like being handed a clean canvas—and I get to start filling it in however I like!

Some years I don't want to change things up too much. But some years I think about total do-overs. Think <u>Extreme ME Makeover</u>. I start by asking myself, "Who do I want to be this year?" Should I go out for a new sport? Learn a new language? Become an international woman of mystery? Is this the year I learn how to code? What about volunteering? I care about animals (especially cute little dogs and cats), the environment (Hello, World!), and I want to help the homeless. Maybe

I should join an organization where I can make a difference in the world! Maybe I should focus on my studies even more and shoot for a boatload of As. Or maybe I should try out a bunch of these options and go for a nice combination platter. Dish it out!
                                                    ^

What I realized as soon as I got to middle school is that ALL these possibilities are open to me come back-to-school time. The best part about starting up a new school year (aside from being with all my friends again) is that I get to try out whatever I want. There's nothing to be scared of. This is an exciting time to explore! If I'm dreaming about doing something, then there's no reason I shouldn't give it a whirl, because there's no better time than now.

Ain't that the truth!

Fashion Sense Matters

There's nothing I love better than a floral dress . . . except maybe Lucas. I 💜 fashion, and picking out what I'm going to wear is my favorite part of every morning. I guess I've always believed that with every item I put on, I'm showing the world who I am, so I take the responsibility very seriously. But I don't care if the clothes are from some fancy designer, a thrift store, or the Internet; it's how I mix, match, put it all together, and, most important, how I WEAR it that makes the difference.

Before I started middle school, my mom mostly chose my outfits for me. But once I got to sixth grade, I wanted to start experimenting with my own individual look. I wanted to rock a fresh style, and for better or for worse (Hello, Harajuku phase!), my mom mostly let me do it. From what I've seen, the people who create their own styles walk around feeling sharp and confident. So I think if you're into trying out a new look, now's a great time to do it.

Preach! lle 39 lle

Trying Out a New Look

For me, getting started was the hardest part, so I hunted around for some tips and advice. I first went to some of my favorite style blogs and YouTube channels, and I discovered there is so much free advice available, it was like commanding my own team of fashionistas! Here's a quick list of what I learned that helped me dress to impress (impress MYSELF, that is!):

1. Buy clothes that fit and make you feel good!

2. Accessories can be your new best friend. (Maya, I still love you, too.)

3. Hats are awesome.

4. Belts rock!

5. Layering lets you wear a few of your favorite pieces at once while creating a whole new look.

So whatever you choose to wear—whether it's fun prints, plaids, trendy colors and patterns, or classic solids—if you wear it with style and an air of confidence, you'll look simply fabulous!

Back-to-School Goals

Here are some general goals Riley and I think are a good start for a great year!

☑ Eat breakfast every day.

☑ Learn something new every day.

☐ Finish a book that wasn't assigned to you.

☑ Make a new friend outside your friend group.

☐ Balance schoolwork and fun extracurriculars.

☑ Decide who you want to be and be that person!

☑ Build your confidence.

☑ Challenge yourself.

Top Secret

Make up your OWN list of back-to-school goals!

Write down some things that you can do to accomplish your goals this year!

Starting Off on the Right Foot

Someone once said, "You never get a second chance to make a first impression." That person happened to be the announcer in a dandruff shampoo commercial— but I think he was right. People of all ages form opinions in the blink of an eye. So it's important that when you set foot in a room, you show people the best you right away.

Now, I don't know about you, but I OCCASIONALLY have a hard time waking up in the morning. Part of me

thinks it's the brightness of the sun that's throwing off my game. (Why must it be so bright, huh? Huh?) But another part of me wonders if waking up is SO hard because I'm not getting as much sleep as I need.

Since I keep hearing about how sleep is "incredibly important" for the brain, how it makes you smarter, more together, and more on top of everything, it's something I KNOW I need to do more of. In fact, I think you and I should make a pledge. We should pledge to sleep more, because to make a great first impression, we need to be on our game and feeling fierce as soon as we walk through those middle school doors!

z z z z z z z z z

44

Maya showed me another way to make a good first impression—walking with confidence. That wasn't so easy for me at first, because I can feel pretty insecure. And besides, how does one walk with confidence? But Maya said that sometimes just ACTING like you're confident is enough to convince people you really are!

So how do you pull off this massive fake-out?

1. Good posture. Straight and not slumped over.

2. A smile. At least have one ready.

3. Good attitude. Think, "Hello, World! I'm gonna do great things."

Here are more ideas I've picked up along the way:

1. Remember, at the beginning of the school year, EVERYONE is nervous—even the coolest of kids. If you can make small talk with people—start a short conversation about anything (the weather, the movie or song of the summer)—you'll break the ice and others will be grateful to you.

2. Be positive! No one likes a downer.

3. And last but SUPER important . . . BE YOU. Just relax. It'll be great!

More about this on the next page!

45

How to Be Award-Winningly Cool

Do you want to be cool? Have you always wondered how all the hip kids do it? Have you bought clothes to look more like them? Pretended to be interested in the stuff they seem to enjoy? Well, as someone who won the Griff-Hawkins Totally Cool Award and has been considered cool since she was popping wheelies in her stroller, Miss Maya's gonna help you out. *Sing it, sister!*

Now lean in. This first piece of advice is killer. . . . Ready?

STOP TRYING SO HARD!

Think about it: have you ever seen a truly cool person working to achieve that air of effortless awesomeness? No, you have not.

Why not?

Good question!

I sure haven't!

Because a cool person is not trying to impress you. A cool person is trying to please himself or herself. Take me, for example. I'm not trying to be anyone else. I DON'T WANT TO BE ANYONE ELSE. I'm content just being me.

Especially during a time in life when everything can turn on a dime—styles, music, which celebrities are hot, which celebrities are not—you don't want to be a slave to "the moment." It's too hard to keep up.

That's why I choose to march to the beat of the drummer in my own head. Fortunately, they happen to be REALLY good at finding the beat. I often ask myself these questions: Is this what I WANT to be doing? Am I blindly following a trend? Am I behaving in a way I'm proud of, or am I doing something because some ding-dong told me to? When it comes down to it, being cool means relying on your own instincts and following your own voice.

COOL

Well put!

Rule the School by Strutting Your Stuff

We all know people who think they're the best. They always believe they're before everyone else, even when they're last in the lunch line. They walk around with their noses in the air and look for rose petals to be thrown at their feet. And though having a good amount of self-confidence is important, these people take it to a whole new level!

Still, it's a good idea to study the behavior of these human peacocks, because even they have a lesson to teach. Peacocks, as we learned in science class, have a knack for attracting attention to themselves. When they want to be noticed, they just strut around and fan out their fabulous tail feathers. They literally put the best part of themselves on display. When I thought about how that could work for me, I realized I didn't need to be quite so over-the-top about it—but if I could shake a tail feather or two, I could make an impression. The world is a more beautiful place because the peacock shares its feathers, and I think the same is true for us when we start showing the world what makes us unique.

Judgments and Assumptions

There's a famous quote that goes: "You can't judge a book by its cover." (Girls, this doesn't apply to your book, which has a beautiful cover.) Anyone who's opened a book and started reading it knows that's true. I happen to believe that you're uniquely qualified to understand this old saying because you're doing some strong work breezing through this great book right now and reading up on some pretty powerful stuff!

Sometimes you'll look at a book cover and think, "Oh, man, I want a piece of whatever's going on in there, because the cover is just sooooo great!" But then— cue horror-movie music—you discover that what's lurking beneath that beautiful cover is the most boring and sleep-inducing stuff since second-period English class! (Please don't tell your English teacher I called her class boring.) The reverse can also be true: boring, plain, simple covers can hide the best and most spine-tingling or heartstring-tugging tales. The bottom line is that you just never know.

So why are we talking about this? Well, because book covers are a good metaphor for life. What's a metaphor, you ask? Clearly someone was snoozing through that boring English class. . . .

Okay, quick teachable moment: a metaphor is a figure of speech that makes a comparison between two wildly different things and points out that they have qualities in common after all. For example, when I say, "Maya's voice is music to Riley's ears," it doesn't mean Maya speaks in song; it means when she speaks, it makes Riley as happy as if she were hearing her favorite song. So that's a metaphor. And when I say, "You can't judge a book by its cover," I also mean that you shouldn't make snap judgments about things based just on their appearances. You have to dig deeper. You have to explore what's beyond that thin front flap.

This applies equally well to the people you encounter, to the assignments you're given, to the activities you're asked to do, to the foods you're asked to try, and to many, many, MANY other things in life. So rather than making a hasty "like" or "dislike" decision, give that person, place, or thing a fair shot. You just might find your new favorite thing in the world.

—Cory

Chapter 3

Look Out, World!
How to Handle Teachers and Homework

School is kind of cool. Anyone who knows me gets I have an interesting relationship with the thing we call "school." By "interesting," I mean it's one of those love-hate deals. There are certain parts of it that I love: seeing my friends, decorating my locker, doing projects in art, getting to help Riley with her problems, and hearing the final bell at the end of the day. There are also parts of school that I dislike with the burning heat of ten thousand suns: homework, tests, lectures, grade grubbing, having to be there every single day, the food in the cafeteria, sweating in gym class, and the sound of the bell at the beginning of the day.

So you probably weren't expecting me to be the one to write the section on school being cool, were you? This definitely seems like something that's much more up my BFF Riley's alley.

Keep reading. . . .

What's Cool About School

When you learn stuff, you get to be part of the conversation. Say someone's arguing that we don't need to protect the environment because there's no such thing as global warming. You can tell that person about a little thing you learned in school called SCIENCE. Then you get to <u>school</u> them on all that you know. *-*-*-*-*

Say you want to be a famous musician. To write your own songs, you need to know how to write poetry, because that's what music is—poetry set to music. And where are you going to learn that, huh? Sing it with me now: schoooool.

Say you want to design video games or develop apps. If that's your bag, you're going to need a foundation in math and computer science. Guess where that foundation's laid?

So even though there are many things about school I don't love, even I can't deny that you can learn a lot there that you need for high school and the real world. For that reason alone, school's pretty cool. But don't go telling Mr. Matthews I said that, okay? I don't want him to get a big head over it (a BIGGER head) and I have a rep to protect!

Cafeteria 101
Where to Sit, What to Eat

When we first got to middle school, Maya and I often had lunch during different periods. That meant we found ourselves walking into the cafeteria all by our lonesomes, facing some pretty gruesome gruel and some gruesomely cruel older kids.

So how do you decide where to sit?

First, look for the friendly faces. Anyone you know from before middle school?

Anyone who seemed nice in one of your new classes?

And there's nothing wrong with introducing yourself to someone you don't know.

It's super easy, in fact. You just open your mouth and say, "Hey, I'm Maya. Can I sit with you?"

Or "Hi! I'm Riley. Mind if I sit down?" Even if the person has saved a seat for another friend, hopefully there will still be some room at the table. But if not, not a big deal. Just find another open spot and try again.

So, what should you eat?

Well, that's really up to you. Whatever makes you feel good and gives you that energy you need to make it through the rest of your day.

Getting Along with Teachers

When you have a dad who's a teacher, you get an early lesson in child-teacher relations. I don't want to say this makes me a pro, but I do have a fair amount of experience in getting along with teachers. That's why I feel pretty qualified to give you the inside scoop on this topic. ✳ ◯ ✳ ◯ ✳ ◯ ✳◯ ✳ ◯ ✳

If there's one thing I hear my dad saying over and over about what makes him crazy, it's when a student doesn't show him respect. When a student shows up late to class, talks during his lessons, pulls out a cell phone, and/or doesn't "do the work" (that's a biggie), these are all things that turn my dad from mild-mannered history teacher into fuming-mad pigeon. That's something you should try to avoid at all costs, believe me! ✳ ◯ ✳ ◯ ✳ ◯ ✳

Now, you may be saying, "Riley, why does this teacher person deserve my respect in the first place? It's not like he or she has done anything to earn it like my friends have."

Of course you're right in that your friends have proven to you that they're worthy. And especially at the start of the school year, when the teacher can barely remember your name, it's hard to understand why you should listen to him or her. But this is one of those things that requires a leap of faith . . . and you're the one who needs to leap first.

If you begin the respect-athon and show your teacher that you trust him or her, you're going to see that respect and trust bounce right back to you from the teach.

Then, once you've got some of that healthy mutual respect going, your teacher is going to show you stuff that you'll be able to use for the rest of your life. That's a pretty good deal if you think about it.

Another thing to keep in mind is that even though your teacher is getting paid to be in school and you're not, he or she could be doing a lot of other things instead. The reason your teacher is there in the first place is because he or she likes the idea of educating students. In short, your teacher wants you to succeed. When you think about it that way, it's probably a little easier to see why you should respect your teacher in the first place, right? So if your teacher's putting in the work, why don't you do both of you a favor and put in your share of the work, too?

What to Do When Your Teacher Fails You

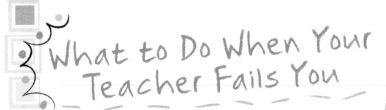

News flash! I've failed tests. And yeah, I did say "tests," plural, as in "more than one." I'd like to be able to tell you that the reason I failed those tests was because I was up late the night before hanging out with my BFF. But the truth is, I failed most of those tests because I didn't study. It's hard to know what the right answers are when you're completely unfamiliar with the questions. Oops . . .

But my worst experience was when I actually DID study and I FAILED ANYWAY. Gah, that was maddening! It made me question why I bothered wasting my time trying when the results would have been the same if I'd just blown it off. But I didn't drop out of school and I didn't stop trying.

Why? Because I learned that failing a test does not mean failing life. It's not that the test (or paper or whatever) is unimportant; it's just that bombing that one test is not the end of the world. It means that I didn't understand whatever concept I was supposed to have learned. So yes, it was a failure, but it turned out to be temporary, because as soon as I saw that bogus grade, I went straight to my teacher, put the test paper down in front of him, and said, "I think this is what we call a cry for help."

I then explained that I really did want to learn the stuff I'd been tested on, but for some reason I hadn't grasped it yet. So once I showed my teacher that I was willing to put in the work, he explained it differently and the whole thing cracked wide open for me.

I also take comfort in this quote: "I have not failed. I've just found ten thousand ways that won't work." You know who said that? A man named Thomas A. Edison. Name ring a bell? He's the guy who invented the lightbulb—you know, that thing that appears above our heads when we get a bright idea! Turns out Edison failed all the time, but that didn't stop him—no, ma'am, no, sir. He kept trying until he found his gajillion-dollar idea. So if ever things start feeling dark for me because I couldn't ace something right away, I think of my man Edison, and the lightbulb in my brain switches back on.

☆ How to Do Your Homework

NICE JOB!

As you know, I'm BIG into homework. I love it. I can't exactly explain why, but I find something incredibly satisfying about tackling an assignment, wrestling it to the ground, and showing it who's boss. That's because I know with each correct answer, my brain is getting stronger and sharper, and my thinking is becoming quicker and more flexible. Once I complete the assignment, I feel like an unstoppable powerhouse!

Since I want you to feel exactly the same way, I've come up with five quick tips that I hope will make the experience more pleasant for you. Just remember that in the end this is going to make you smarter and more interesting—and, as Dad always says, "No pain, no gain!"

1. Pick a good time to get the work done. Since I do a lot of extracurricular activities, the afternoon isn't an ideal homework time for me. That's why I always plan to tackle my assignments right after we finish dinner. I take my dessert back to my desk with me so I can have a sweet treat while toughing it out.

2. Have a designated homework spot. Your "homework hut" should be comfortable but not TOO comfortable, because you don't want to risk falling asleep. You want this to be a place that puts you in a good mood and where all your supplies and books are at arm's length.

3. Work harder on the hard stuff. Unlike people, all homework is not created equal. Some of it is outrageously hard. And guess what? That's the stuff you should devote more of your time to, because once you master it, it won't bother you again.

$$\frac{\sqrt{3}}{4} = (a^2) \quad \Sigma_n \cong 6$$
$$\frac{1}{2} = b \quad \frac{1}{x} + \frac{1}{y} \quad \sqrt{11-x}$$
$$\pi = 3.14$$
$$2 \times \frac{17}{5}$$
$$\left(\frac{1}{xy}\right) + x^2$$

KEEP IT UP!

4. When you need to, ask for help. Sometimes homework is a bear! If that's the case and you've tried your hardest to solve it on your own, ask for help. There's no reason you should struggle forever.

5. Think long-term. Now that you're in middle school, your teachers will occasionally assign big long-term projects. These can be really fun learning experiences and prepare you for the stuff you're going to see in high school (woo-hoo!). But these projects can also become a nightmare if you don't budget your time right and discover you have a massive report due in two days. So when you get a long-term assignment, set aside a certain period of time every day to work on it and attack it in bite-sized chunks. That way it never seems overwhelming, and you'll have plenty of time to make it amazing!

AMAZING WORK ♥

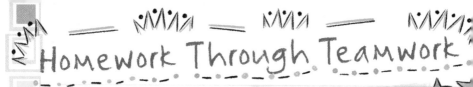

Homework Through Teamwork

Riley and I are similar in a lot of ways. Our love of homework is not one of them! So instead of asking Riley to do my homework for me (as much as I know she'd love to!), I suggested the next best thing: doing our homework together. Much to my surprise, it not only turned out to be fun, but I may have even learned something in the process!

There are a lot of good reasons to work together in groups. For one thing, if one of you (meaning me) gets stuck on a problem, the other person can help explain how it's done—hopefully in a way that makes it understandable. For another, if the homework involves coming up with an argument for or against something, the more heads working together the more perspectives and ideas you'll have. Finally, if you have to spend your time doing homework—and let's face it, even the best of us do—having a friend to sit with makes the process a lot less stressful.

Extreme Homework Tips from Farkle

Well hello, Dolly! It is I, the Farkle, at your service. Because my two favorite ladies, Riley and Maya, have asked me to share some of my best homework advice, I am here to drop some knowledge on you.

Now get your pencils out and get ready to write fast, because Farkle moves with the speed of a cheetah and the grace of a gazelle that's about to be eaten by that cheetah.

Tip #1: Do it early and do it often. Like Farkle always says, "Practice makes perfect," so I advise practicing homework even when it isn't assigned.

Tip #2: Get rid of all distractions. No TV. No phone. No computer (unless it's part of the assignment). No music. No talking! And if you want to do the Full Farkle: no windows. I told you this was EXTREME! Daydreaming is dangerous, and once you picture yourself strolling outside holding hands with Riley and Maya, there's no way in the world you'll be able to finish that assignment.

Tip #3: Be a genius! This makes homework a breeze, and as a genius myself, I can't recommend it highly enough.

What's Your Study Style?

1. When do you start working on a big paper?
    A. The day it's assigned!
    B. A few days before it's due.
    C. Night before it's due—the pressure helps me!

2. Getting an A is:
    a. the only outcome I'll accept.
    b. supercool!
    c. I'll let you know if it ever happens.

3. I use the library to:
    a. do deep research.
    b. get some homework done.
    c. hide from my mom—it's the last place she'd look.

4. Taking notes in class:
    a. is the best way to understand and learn materials.
    b. is what the teacher tells us to do.
    c. is the best way to communicate with my friends.

5. When taking a quiz:
    a. I recall everything I learned from studying all week.
    b. I think about each answer and try my best.
    c. I answer C for each question (including this one).

Score:
Give yourself 5 points for every A response, 3 for every b, and 1 for every C response.

5-9: Sup, slacker? You use school as a place to get educated, but not necessarily about academic subjects. Though you're happy to study a magazine for the latest styles and celebrity gossip, it isn't going to get you an A.

10-17: Salutations, solid student! You might not be at the top of your class or ace your tests, but you always turn in decent work, and that's good enough for you!

18-25: Howdy, hotshot! Clear off some space on the mantel, because you work hard and get results. With your A+ study habits, you're a study ace!

Cory's Assignment

Okay, okay, I know I said I wasn't going to keep butting in to Maya and Riley's book, but I have an assignment that you're going to love (I think . . .). On any given weekend day, I want you to team up with your best friend and spend the whole day without using your phones or computers. Plan a day full of activities, and when you get back, try writing about your experiences together. Riley, Maya, Farkle, and Lucas wound up loving it, so I bet you will, too!

FROM THE DESK OF CORY MATTHEWS

Top Secret

Now, we know what you're thinking: "An assignment?! Really?! I didn't read this book to get more homework!" We'd feel the same way. In fact, we did when we were given this assignment. I mean, give up technology? What are you, crazy?! But in the end, we actually really liked it, and we suggest you give it a shot, too! Start by making a list below of all the things you'd like to do that don't involve technology.

Okay, to take a page from Dad's book (or rather, a page of his from OUR book), grab your bestie, leave your technology at home, and go out and try some of the things on your list. Then write about your adventures below. Did you have fun? What was your favorite part of being without technology? What did you miss the most? So . . . would you do it again?!

Detention

Detention blows. It's like being in prison . . . except you're still at school . . . after everyone else has left. There really isn't anything good to say about it, so I'm having a hard time coming up with some positive spin on this for you. But if you did the crime, you do the time.

While you're trapped in the penalty box, you might as well use the time to do something worthwhile. Like sketching. Or writing a note to your bestie. Or coming up with an idea for a movie. Or writing a song.

Or, if you must, just suck it up and do your homework. At least that way, once you've earned your freedom back, you've gotten it out of the way and won't have to wreck your precious home time that night with schoolwork.

Eventually, you will get out of detention, so I guess there is good news after all!

Chapter 4

A World of Possibilities!
What to Do About Extracurriculars

"Extracurricular" is a long word. It's also a word that's difficult to spell. What does it mean exactly? Truthfully, we had no idea. We learned in English that "curricular" comes from the word "curriculum." Now do you get it?

Yeah, that didn't help us, either. Then Farkle explained that "curriculum" means the classes and educational stuff a school offers. So "extracurricular" means the fun stuff you do after school that may or may not be educational. Since it's not part of the regular school day, it's an added bonus—an extra, if you please!

If you think about it, there are a lot of pros to extracurriculars.

There's an awesome kind of freedom in not having to go directly home from school. You don't have to deal with annoying siblings. You can steer clear of meddling parents. And best of all, you get to hang out with your friends longer while doing something fun.

In other words, win-win-win!

Get Involved!

As previously discussed, I'm the enthusiastic type. When I go shopping, I try on everything in my size. When I draw, I use every colored pencil in the box. When I bake, I get every surface of the kitchen dirty. Because I'm strong and energetic, I feel like I should try to do everything I can before I get too old and tired (a.k.a. age 22). So you can only imagine how excited I was when I got to middle school and suddenly a whole world of after-school activities opened up to me.

At first I signed up and tried out for everything. But I soon discovered that plan couldn't work, because a lot of the activities met at the same time. Also, when I finally got home, I was so tired from all the running around that I could barely do my homework. It turned out to be an unexpected (and sort of unpleasant) lesson in time management. So, since I've already gone through the pain of this, let me tell you what I've learned so far about the game of extracurriculars.

The first thing you should do is take a look at your options. Often you'll find on the school website a listing of the teams and clubs offered. If you can't find a specific list, write up your own list of some activities you might want to do. They'll basically fall into three major categories:

Sports   Academic   Artistic

Sports usually divide into three seasons: fall, winter, and spring. Depending on how sporty you are, you can pick out one new sport for each of the seasons. For example, you could play soccer in the fall, basketball in the winter, and softball in the spring. But you should pick whatever's most fun for you. Also, don't forget that some sports, like gymnastics and ballet, aren't necessarily offered at school but can run throughout the year. o o o o o o o o o

The more academic clubs, like the tech club, environmental club, knowledge bowl, sign language club, math team, 4-H club, and allies for diversity, can be really terrific to be a part of, too. But your school may have other options as well, so if you can't find a listing of them on your school's website or up on the ol' school corkboard, it's worth asking a teacher or guidance counselor where you can learn more about them. That's the kind of question that will make your guidance counselor's whole day, because that's the guidance counselor's job: to help guide you and make your school experience even better.

Finally, don't forget that there are also plenty of activities you can do to entertain your creative side. Your school might have a jazz band, improv comedy troupe, photography club, yearbook club, book club, movie club, cooking club. . . . The possibilities here are endless. And if your school doesn't have a club to suit one of your interests, maybe you'll want to consider starting one yourself!

I'M Sketchy... Literally

I'm a drawer. (Pssst... I think you mean you're a draw-er, not a drawer—because if you're a drawer, you're something people put their socks in.)

↳ A drawer

(Whoops! Good catch, my genius friend. Thanks for the correction. Def not how I want to be known.)

Me →

Take two: I'm an artist. I started drawing pictures as a little kid. I always loved how I could sketch out a few lines and turn what I saw in front of me into a creation of my own.

Now, even though I'm not what anyone would call a serious student, art inspires me. That's why I've tried to learn as much as I can about some of my heroes like Pablo Picasso. Picasso had this amazing artistic education—it helped that his father, like Riley's, was a teacher—but he did a lot of learning outside the classroom, too.

Picasso once said, "Learn the rules like a pro, so you can break them like an artist." Even though I'm more of a breaking-the-rules type than a following-the-rules type, I get his point.

See, when it comes to art, there are lots of ways for you to get an education, and they don't all require school. In fact, I learned from my subway buddy, Crazy Hat, that there's a whole group of people known as "Outsider Artists" who never got any formal training at all. She said they just created works of art that flowed from their souls. Then they practiced, doing piece after piece until they found a style that worked for them.

That's one of the things I love best about art. There's no wrong way to do it. You just go with what you feel, and the rest will follow!

When I ran for student body government back in the day, Maya was my campaign manager. Since we were able to run in any form of government we chose, I ran for princess, Farkle ran for dictator, and Lucas ran for president.

VOTE FARKLE
FOR LEADERSHIP
FOR CHANGE
FOR DICTATOR

Maya and I are both thinking about running for student government again this year. We're running for different jobs, of course, and that way we can help each other campaign. The first thing we need to do is come up with some slogans, so we're going to create a list of possibilities for each other.

Vote for Princess Riley

72

My Slogans for Riley

Time to Get Rile-d Up! Vote for Riley!

Riley's Got Rhythm, Riley's Got Style,
Riley's Your Girl, She'll Win by a Mile!

Matthews Means
Business: Vote Riley!

Vote Right.
Vote Riley!

My Slogans
for Maya

In Our Hearts,
Hart's Our Girl!

Hart's Got Heart—
Vote Maya!

Maya's My-a Choice for Student Council!

Maya's Hart-Stoppingly Good!

Rebel with a Cause: Maya Hart for
Student Government!

LUCAS
FOR
PRESIDENT
'Preciate Your Vote!

☆ Write a Totally Cool Slogan!

Now you go ahead and write a slogan for your BFF, and she or he will write yours!

The Sky's the Limit

As you know, my dad teaches history. The man LOVES history. He totally geeks out when it comes to talking about the dates and locations of various battles. He's read more presidential biographies than there have been presidents. And when it comes to the Civil War, he'll dress up like a Union soldier for a reenactment and pretend he's just come off the battlefield. Like I said, he TOTALLY geeks out. But even though his obsession makes NO sense to me, Mom encourages him because she says she likes that he has a hobby. (I think she likes it because when he's busy with his hobby she gets the afternoon to relax!)

But one of the cool things about having a hobby—be it doing something with your hands (like knitting or woodworking), playing a game that's competitive (like cards or chess) or solitary (like Sudoku or crossword puzzles), or maybe even shopping—is that it encourages you to spend time doing something you absolutely love. Hobbies don't require anyone else's approval. They're for you to enjoy for as long as you like!

That might sound dorky—and the truth is, a lot of people think other people's hobbies ARE dorky—but having a hobby means you get to do something that tickles your fancy. Do yourself a favor and give the Goldilocks method a shot: try out a bunch of different things until you find one that's JUST RIGHT for you. (You'll know it's right when you're doing that thing and you lose track of time because you've been having so much fun!)

H o b b i e s

R o c k

Venturing into the Real World

When the two of us are together, one of the things we love to do is explore the world around us. We're lucky because we live in what we think is the most exciting city in the world, New York City. I call it "the center of the universe," and I call it "the city that never sleeps" (especially on garbage day). Because our hometown has so much to offer, during the weekends and summer breaks, we like to pretend we're tourists here and check out all the things the city is famous for in the first place.

For instance, one of the things that comes to mind when we think about New York is the Statue of Liberty. When immigrants arrived by ship in the United States, she served as the welcoming committee for the newcomers, greeting them with her outstretched arm and epic nature.

Though we'd seen her from afar, we knew we needed to get up close and personal with Lady Liberty to check her out. That's when we decided to head to Liberty Island and take a tour. It was awesome! Not only did we get to see the great green lady herself, but we also went over to Ellis Island and checked out an archive that gave us insight into the lives of our ancestors when they first came to America.

Field Trips Rock!

Say you don't live in New York. We're sure there are still a lot of cool places in whatever city, town, or village you call home. You might have already visited some or most of your town's hot spots. But we'll bet that even if you think you've seen EVERYTHING your area has to offer, there are still some secret locations you haven't yet discovered. Your mission, should you choose to accept it, is to find those places and explore them! Why? Because the more you know about where you're from, the more interesting YOU become. Even if you think your town isn't that exciting, there are interesting and wonderful people to meet and things to see no matter where you are.

You can also venture out by escaping to the great outdoors, or what we city slickers hear is called "nature." For some, this could mean the beach; for others, the woods and the mountains. Truthfully, we're not experts on this topic, since the only places we've ever camped out have been each other's apartments.

Finally, if you really want to venture out, you might consider getting an after-school job of some sort. (It'd also be a good way to make a little extra spending money.) You're probably not quite old enough to work in a store or restaurant, but think about opening your own business— say, selling muffins like we did—and then introducing your product to the people of your community or setting up a website and selling it around the globe!

Just remember: it's YOUR world now, and we want you to meet it with open eyes, a clear mind, and a full heart!

Go on a cool and kooky mini adventure, and write about what you did.

Explore your world!

me

TICKET

ONE WAY 000000

0015 OO

78

When I when

Which Extracurriculars Are Right for YOU?

Pick three of your favorite activities:

Math club (1)
Soccer (2)
Cheerleading (2)
Yearbook (3)
Debate club (1)
Student Council (3)
Newspaper (3)
Volleyball (2)
Softball (2)

Band/orchestra (1)
Theater (3)
Dance (2)
Art club (3)
Basketball (2)
Chorus (3)
Gymnastics (2)
Track and field (2)

Now add up the numbers next to your top three activities.

Score:

3-4: You're all about academics and try to keep your number one muscle—your brain—in the best shape possible. Send us a postcard from the Ivy League, will ya?

5-7: You're a serious jock, you varsity high school athlete-to-be! If you keep up the training, there'll be no stopping you.

8-9: You're the social glue of the school. You're the artist-in-residence and the civic-minded memory keeper. Whatever's going on, you know the skinny.

80

Chapter 5

You Rock My World!

All About Crushes

We've all seen it happen. One minute you're walking down the hall, having a great conversation with your friend, and the next, they go quiet and become a googly-eyed drooler.

I can't imagine such a thing, but go on, Maya!

What happened was THE CRUSH appeared.

The Crush [pronounced OH EM GEE!!! YAAAAAASSSS!!!] - (n.) a person who makes the heart go BOOM! BOOM! BOOM!

When The Crush comes into your life, a lot of stuff is pushed to the side so that body, soul, and brain can give their full attention to this dazzling object of desire. You'll probably spend the day thinking about the person you believe is going to be the love of your life. And you'll probably wind up doing something that will majorly embarrass you as you try to get that person's attention.

I can attest!

In this chapter we'll do our best to help you deal with having and managing your crush, because we know from our own experiences what it's like to crush hard.

And we know it's not always pretty!

All You Need to Know About Boys and Girls

In life, in subways, and especially in middle school, people spend a lot of time talking about the differences between boys and girls. "Boys be all like THIS. And girls be all like THAT." Check, got it, thanks. But in my time on planet Earth, I've noticed a few things. When people—either girls or boys—are in crush mode, they're ALL thinking, "Please, PLEASE notice me. Please see me for the amazing person I am. Please know that I, and I alone, possess the power to make your heart smile and that together we can take on the world and live happily ever after." They're also thinking, "We will look SO great holding hands as we walk into the school dance together." Last, they hope that they don't do something that will make The Crush run away screaming.

When it comes to the basics, like what's going on in the crusher's heart (a.k.a. the Chamber of Secrets), the reality is, girls and boys aren't all that different.

Follow Your Heart

Love you, Mom!

First love can be the best feeling in the whole world. It can make you feel like you're on a mountain high, twirling around and singing in a way that would make the von Trapp family jealous. It can also make you feel like you've fallen into a deep, dark cave and you can't see anything or find your way back out to the light. A lot of the time, it can make you feel both of these things in the space of the same day.

From this point on in your life, your heart is going to be sending you lots of signals. Sometimes they'll be joyous and wonderful, and sometimes they'll stink and make you want to cry. But remember that your heart is strong, and it will see you through both the good and bad times. So keep it open to possibilities, trust that it will guide you, and don't be afraid to follow where it leads!

Topanga

Flirting: Fake It Till You Make It

I've heard there's an art to flirting. If that's the case, my early efforts at flirting with Lucas would probably best be described as . . . primitive. As I watched Missy,

another girl in my class, flirt with him, I felt like a finger painter competing with Leonardo da Vinci! I tried to flirt with Lucas, but I just wound up embarrassing myself (and everyone around me). In short, I felt like a failure at flirting.

But wanting—scratch that—NEEDING to do better, I started studying the masters. These were people so smooth in the way they expressed body language, it was like they'd been studying it as a second language since kindergarten. The number one thing they did? They smiled!

A little scientific research confirmed that a person immediately becomes more attractive by smiling.

Exhibit A!

The great flirters also had good eye contact with The Crush. They kept throwing glances in their crush's direction, which showed The Crush that they were interested in what he or she was saying and doing. They also might reach out and lightly touch The Crush's arm or shoulder. They were never too grabby about it (Unwanted touching = not okay!), but a well-timed gesture can silently say, "I think you're awesome."

Another thing Pro-Flirters (P.F.s for short) do is compliment their crushes. They avoid creepy compliments like the ones that focus on some part of the person's body (because ewww, calling out a person's body parts is awkward). But effective compliments are still crush-specific. For example, the P.F. points out something The Crush is wearing, then says he or she always looks stylish, or the P.F. brings up something smart or funny The Crush said and mentions how it was such a perfect line. Effective compliments are also genuine. Only say it if you actually mean it. P.F.s also know the importance of listening: they want to know what The Crush has to say, what he or she is up to, and how he or she is feeling that day.

TRUST ME, I know it's a physical impossibility to remain calm, cool, and collected when you're standing anywhere near your crush. But if you use any of the lessons I learned from the Pro-Flirters at my school, I hope they'll help you "fake it till you make it."

PS: Don't forget to smile! 85

Getting Ready for a First Date

Well, friend, you did it! Just by being you (and possibly by using some of Riley's great flirting tips), you scored a date with Hottie McHeyGirl. You are officially the envy of all your friends—probably your whole school. And though getting to the point where someone asked you out (or where you asked someone out) once seemed like the biggest deal ever, now you have a new reality to deal with: going on that first date! In other words, YOU, MEET DATING WORLD. ♥ - - - ♥ - - - ♥ - - - ♥

From what I've seen with Riley, especially when you're just starting to date, rolling with a group can be helpful. Basically, having a friend along takes the pressure off the two lovebirds to make all the conversation themselves. Sure, some of you won't have a problem with that because you're champion chatters. But even if you're one of those who can gab nonstop, you might feel a little tongue-tied when it's just you and your date, sitting in a tree. . . .

So what are some things you can do to prepare? There's the obvious stuff, like outfit selection and primping. We'll get more into primping later, but do everyone a favor and shower before you go out. Most people sweat more when they get nervous—better to start out daisy fresh than adding stink on top of stink. As for what to wear, there is only one absolute must—and it's not "must buy new wardrobe" or "must wear most expensive outfit I own." It's "must be comfy."

What I mean by "Must be comfy" is that you need to find an outfit that makes you feel great. You want to be wearing something that's not too big and not too small. It should feel just right. You also want to make sure that you're not sporting formal wear if you're being taken to (or taking your date to) a bowling alley, or wearing a bowling shirt if you're going to a nice dinner. Try to get some idea of where you're going and what you're doing so you know how FAHN-CY you should be.

Don't forget, if you're feeling nervous, chances are your date's feeling pretty nervous, too. In fact, let's just assume that your date's WAY more nervous than you so you can start feeling better and more at ease. If you show your date that you're feeling calm, you'll set the example and that will chill him or her out, which will lead to less awkwardness all around.

Oh! And here's another thing: if someone asked you on a date, even though you may expect that person to pay for you, sometimes this ain't gonna be the case. And since you don't really know what he or she has in the ol' wallet, it's best to be smart and bring some of your own cash along in case your date doesn't have the money to cover the price of your admission or what you ate. My mom calls this "mad money." But even if you don't have mad cash, it's better to be safe than sorry!

And if you were the asker, you could offer to pay for your date. Or simply ask if splitting the bill is okay. It's usually the way to go!

Love Notes to Riley and Maya

Didja miss me? What a ridiculous question! Of course you missed me. But don't worry—Captain Farkle's back just in time to help steer this love boat into clear waters. What time is it, you ask? It's Farkle time!

As someone who's been in love with both Riley and Maya since FOREVER, I have a pretty good understanding of how this love stuff works. That's because my heart has been shot full of Cupid's arrows. I think if you're in love with someone, you should let that person know. After all, what's the point in keeping it to yourself? That'd be like building an incredible diorama and not bringing it into class to show off. In other words: crazy.

The Farkle method of declaring your love to your crush (or in my case, CRUSHES) is to write a note. But rather than just describe such a note to you, I thought I'd share two of mine—as you know, I like an audience! (Riley, Maya—I love you.)

Riley, Riley, Riley, Riley,
Even saying your name makes me smiley.
Your beauty, your style, and your natural grace,
All work together to make my heart race.
If we were together, I'd be the luckiest Farkle in the land—
It'd be even better than my dream of being in a boy band.
Riley, please date me and be my girlfriend.
If you say no, it will be my end.
I'll lose my faith in the universe—
My tendency to geek out will get even worse.
But if you say yes to a date with me,
You'll make me as happy as happy can be.
Riley, you're a star, and I think you sparkle—
You make me want to be a better Farkle.

xoxo,
Farkle

My Dearest Maya,

How do I love thee? Let me count the ways: 1, 2, 3, 4, 5, 6, 7, 8, 9, 10! I could go on and on, but since you and I are both perfect tens, that seemed like overkill. You may question my love, but Maya, know that I would even eat bitter chocolate for you. Not a lot, but definitely a little. In short, forget hydrogen, baby, you're my number one element!

Yours forever and always,
Farkle

Top Secret

If someone really, really, REALLY likes you and writes you love notes and texts, and you're just not feeling it (Farkle . . . cough . . .), the worst thing that you can do is give No Text Back (or as Riley and I like to call it, the old N.T.B.). You 99.9 percent of the time owe it to your admirer to be honest by letting them know in a nice way that you're not interested. A polite "thanks but no thanks" text is best. It might be hard for your admirer to hear, but nothing's worse than radio silence! Come up with some kind responses below:

PS: And if they still don't stop contacting you, then it's okay to ignore.

Love is in the air! Write a list of all the qualities you look for in a crush. Swoon!

What to Do When Your ➡ Crush Has a <u>Crush</u>

You've heard the gossip through the grapevine that your crush has a crush. And for a minute, you think, "YESSSSSSSS! My dream has come true! Crush has finally come to realize that I am their one and only!" It's one of those moments that happy dances were made for!

But just as you're about to break into a dance of joy, you hear part two of the gossip: the tragic conclusion. It turns out that your crush isn't crushing on YOU. They are actually crushing on someone else.

What do you do when you get news this . . . crushing?
I've broken it down into a few steps that I hope will help:

<u>Step 1:</u> Eat ice cream. One, it's a sweet treat and comfort eat, and it will just make you feel better. Two, if you eat it quickly enough, it will give you a brain freeze, which will temporarily stop you from thinking about . . . The Crush.

<u>Step 2:</u> Scratch Step 1. You shouldn't eat to feel better. Instead, go through your yearbook and find someone you find cute. Even though switching feelings to a new crush isn't going to be a snap, Old Crush has proven to be a dud, and New Crush could be amazing!

<u>Step 3:</u> Okay, scratch Step 2. Jump into a new crush only if it happens organically. What you should really do is take a look at yourself in the mirror and remind yourself that <u>YOU. ARE. TERRIFIC.</u> You're beautiful inside and out. You've got a great personality. And know that even though you're not in your crush's sights right now, at some point that person's going to wake up, smell the coconut water, and feel like a dum-dum for letting you get away! But by then, you'll be on your next adventure, with or without a new boo!

Seventh-Grade Spring Fever

-A Note from Cory

In Mark Twain's classic <u>Tom Sawyer, Detective</u>, Huck Finn explains the concept of spring fever to his friend Tom by saying, "It's spring fever. That is what the name of it is. And when you've got it, you want—oh, you don't quite know what it is you do want, but it just fairly makes your heart ache, you want it so!" I think we all know what he was REALLY talking about here. . . . So how do you cure this "fever"? Try these remedies:

I hope you enjoy our artwork!

Exercise.
Do it early and do it often!

Fly a kite.

Ride a bike.

Dance.

Plant a garden.

Sketch.

Meditate.

Daydream.

Do yoga.

93

How Hard Are You Crushing?

1. How do you describe your crush?
   - a. Better looking than any celebrity I've seen.
   - b. Kind, funny, amazing.
   - c. Most popular kid in school.

2. Do you know your crush's schedule on a daily basis?
   - a. From the first bell in the morning to the last bell.
   - b. We have lunch the same period most days.
   - c. Is that even a real question? Duh, of course I do!

3. If I don't see my crush:
   - a. I'll think about them and check their Instagram.
   - b. my day isn't quite as happy.
   - c. I'll message them to make sure they're okay.

4. The best thing my crush could do for me is:
   - a. realize that I exist!
   - b. smile at me.
   - c. buy me jewelry.

5. The feelings that I have for my crush:
   - a. are not the same as what they feel for me . . . yet!
   - b. get even stronger when I spend more time with them.
   - c. change with what they wear.

Score:

Mostly As: Danger zone! Your feelings are so intense you can barely see straight. But never forget how awesome you are, and if your crush doesn't know you're alive, they might not be worthy of your love (or even your time spent thinking about them).

Mostly Bs: Though you have a good crush going, you're not going to let it crush you. So show the object of your affection some love: smile and look them in the eye when you speak. A little positivity can go a long way!

Mostly Cs: It's possible you like your crush more for their popularity than for their personality. So before you spend any more time obsessing, really think about who they are, what they're like, and how they treat you and those around you. If you wind up liking what you see, keep on crushing!

Chapter 6

The World Is Full of Life Lessons!

Making the Best of Family Life

There was once a time in my life when everything was perfect. The sun would always shine. My skin was always clear. I didn't have a care in the world. Then disaster struck: my brother, Auggie, was born.

Suddenly, my peaceful world was shattered. The house looked like a tornado hit it. My parents went crazy. And I was no longer the center of their world.

But Dad quickly reminded me that life's full of challenges—whether you're an older sibling or a younger one. He told me that younger siblings have to get used to hand-me-downs, leftovers, and lots of advice. He went on to explain that having a sibling and being part of a bigger family was a fact of life for me and Auggie. It wasn't something that was going to change or that we could simply wish away.

The Perks of Siblings!

Instead of looking at the negatives of the sibling situation, Dad told me that I needed to focus on all the positives (which I'm usually oh so good at)! Fortunately, because he knows me pretty well, Dad made me a list.

"Why a Big Family Rocks"

1) Parents no longer have time to pry into your business, since their attention is divided.

2) If something goes wrong, you can blame it on your sibling.

3) If you need a partner for something, you can usually get your sibling to join you.

4) Younger sibs will idolize you.

5) Older siblings will protect you.

CORY   TOPANGA
RILEY   AUGGI
MAYA

I've got to hand it to Dad; he did a pretty good job of convincing me to make the best of family life. Most importantly, he taught me that being a sibling—younger or older—can be tough but that more family means more to love!

How to Be an Awesome Sibling

Because I'm older, it's important for me to set a good example for my brother. For instance, I've learned that if I offer to help Mom set the table, I'm showing Auggie how to behave. When you behave in the way you want a person to act and they start following your lead, it's called modeling.
So, yes, I am officially a role model!

As a role model, I also pave the road with Mom and Dad so that they can make Auggie's life a little easier.

Younger siblings have responsibilities to their older siblings, too. When your older sibling asks your parent(s) for things—extending curfews, giving more allowance, setting them free—always have your older sibling's back. Trust me, kids. It'll benefit you in the long run.

Siblings know each other their whole lives. So being decent to each other and sticking together is a much better plan than falling apart!

Being an Only Child Rocks

I'm not going to go on about the misery of siblings, since it seems to be pretty obvious to anyone with eyes, ears, and a nose. So what I'm going to do is tell you why being a "one and only" is amazing.

1. You don't have to share—anything! You aren't fighting over food, clothes, or space. If the thing exists, it's yours for the taking.

2. The only messes you have to clean up are the ones you make yourself.

3. Parents are never bored by you. They'll never flash you the "been there, done that" expression, because with you, it's all new.

4. Parents don't know all the tricks. That's related to number three, but the twist is that you can pull a lot of stuff on them that they won't know to expect.

5. You don't have to live up to anyone's example but your own.

In other words, you lucky duck, it's all about YOU!

Living with One Parent

I love hanging out with Riley and her family. Being with them is like being at a circus; nonstop action and entertainment, parents who somehow seem to be everywhere, and the sounds of a noisy child wailing.

Life in my apartment is a lot different. It's just Mom and me (and Gammy Hart, too). And Mom isn't even around all that much, because she's working hard to support us. Since I don't have the "joy" of living with siblings, I wind up getting a lot of time to myself. People ask if I get lonely, and sometimes I do—but mostly I love having the time and space to myself to do what I want. What I've discovered is that if I make a schedule for myself—assigning a certain amount of time for after-school snacking, exercising, magazine reading, blog scanning, iChatting, and TV watching (with some spontaneous dance breaks thrown in)—the late afternoon and evening fly by.

Whether you have no parents or a dozen, family is what you make of it. You can't choose your family, but you can pick friends like Riley who become family.

Are YOU a Good Sibling?

1. When you see your sibling in the morning, what do you do?

   a. Grumble good morning. (2)

   b. Yell, "Get out of the bathroom!" (1)

   c. Offer them the last pancake. (3)

2. When you get into a fight, how does it usually end?

   a. With tears and hurt feelings. (1)

   b. With a hug—we can't stay mad at each other for long. (3)

   c. With a parent deciding we're both wrong. (2)

3. Do you usually get your sibling a present on his or her birthday?

   a. I write "happy birthday" on my sib's Facebook wall. (2)

   b. Of course! (3)

   c. If I remember . . . and haven't spent all my money. (1)

4. Do you play games or do activities with your sibling?

   a. Bingo! And I usually wind up having fun. (3)

   b. Not unless I'm forced. (1)

   c. Sometimes. (2)

5. When my sibling's upset, I . . .

   a. try to make him or her feel better. (3)

   b. let him or her get the bigger cookie for dessert. (2)

   c. think, "Whatever, not my problem!" (1)

5-7: It's possible that you like your socks more than you like your sibling. But hopefully they'll grow out of this awful stage and you can be friends later.

7-12: You and your sib have your ups and downs, but you basically get along. The bottom line is that when push comes to shove (as long as you're not doing the shoving), you always have each other's backs!

13-15: Awesome is the best way to describe this relationship. You rely on each other and genuinely like each other. So not only are you good siblings to each other, but you're also great friends.

Score:

100

The Makings Of a Good Babysitter

If you want me to like you as a babysitter, here's what you should do:

1. Be on time! If you're late, my parents freak out, and that freaks me out.

2. Be FUN!

3. Be in a good mood!

4. Pay attention to ME, not your phone!

5. Treats—give them to me early and often!

6. Play with me!

7. Don't let me get too crazy!

8. Tell me about cool stuff!

9. Be patient with me. I'll get it eventually!

10. Let me stay up a little—just a little—past my bedtime!

AUGGIE

Keeping and Negotiating Curfews

Little-known fact: when you get to middle school, your long-standing War on Bedtime will suddenly become the far more explosive War on Curfew. You should know that these wars have been raging for hundreds if not thousands of years. So get ready.

Let's discuss!
What's the purpose of a curfew?

Opinions differ, so we'll present both ideas and let you decide!

<u>Opinion 1</u>: Curfews were invented to keep kids safe. When the "must-be-home-by-9:00 P.M." rule is in effect, the chances of running into trouble outside starting at 9:01 drop to zero. Also, you'll be safe from vampires.

<u>Opinion 2</u>: Curfews were invented to ruin your fun! Since all the more interesting things start later, by forcing a kid to go home at a certain (early) hour, a parent is basically trying to make sure their child will miss out on the cool stuff!

So what happens if your parent(s) tell you that you must be home WAY earlier than you'd like?

Since we've hit this roadblock ourselves, allow us to tell you about the dos and don'ts as we've experienced them!

We initially discovered two ways to handle curfew issues. The first was to ignore the curfew entirely.

The second was to follow it blindly and sometimes even get home early. Neither is ideal, and that's why we hit on another option—what we like to call "Door # 3."

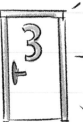

Door #3 is also called "The Art of the Deal." First thing you have to do is tell your parent(s) you think they have some good points and you'd like to discuss them.

You'll need to be calm, cool, and collected, because if you start to get emotional and shouty, they'll stop listening and you'll never get what you want. Now keep in mind, because your parent(s) are so old, they probably have a lot more experience wheeling and dealing than you do. That's why you need to come to the table prepared: make sure you have a good list of reasons why you need to stay out later, how you plan to stay safe, and how your being able to come home at the hour you'd like will help make you a better person. Parents love that stuff. Trust us.

Also keep a few don'ts in mind. Don't resort to name-calling. Don't say, "You just don't understand" (because they do, even if they won't admit it). Don't threaten them by saying, "You don't think I'm responsible? I'll show you irresponsible!" If you do that, chances are they'll never let you out.

DOS

DON'TS

So simply explain that though you know they're only looking out for you, you want to show them how responsible you really are!

Life Lessons

One of the things we've learned over the years is that our family is absolutely the most important thing in our lives. We love one another. We care about one another. We want the best for one another. But sometimes, in the craziness of our day-to-day lives, we don't take the time to show our family members how we feel. Because we get rushed and busy, we wind up taking them for granted. We forget how much they're doing that actually makes our lives easier and better on a daily basis, and we don't thank them for their work.

If we can give you one piece of advice that will make you and the people who love you happier, we think it's this: take a few minutes each day to think about what you're grateful for, and then express that gratitude to the people making it happen. So if the note your mom put in your lunch made you smile, thank her for it. The thank-you will make

Thank you!

her smile, too . . . and it will also let her know that you appreciate her efforts. If your dad helped you with some homework and made it easier for you to complete your assignment, be sure to tell him that.

The girls once got an assignment to teach them a special lesson on appreciation. Riley and Maya spent some time working in the cafeteria and discovered what a tough job it really is. When they were finished, you better believe they were thankful for the people who work there on a daily basis. It turns out the people who think about what's good in their lives and then express their gratitude are usually the happiest and most satisfied people around. Wouldn't you want to be part of that group?

So we'll end this by saying thank you for reading this and thank you for being your best you!

—Cory
and Topanga

Top Secret

Dinner talk! One of our favorite things to do over the dinner table is discuss our days. My family loves to hear every single detail about everything in my day. *DO THEY?!* Dinner is one of the few times for families to sit down and have a moment together. It's nice to share what's happening in our lives.

Oh, don't forget to ask your parent(s) about their day. They're people, too! Plus, they might remember how nice you were the next time you ask for a later curfew!

Make a list of a few funny stories about your day today to share with your family!

We R Family

No family is perfect, but ideally there is kindness and respect. and LOVE!
If your family is driving you crazy, remember that your best friends are like a family that you choose, and you can count on them, too.

Chapter 7

Ready or Not, World Here I Come!
Rocking Social Situations

Oh, peer pressure—what is your deal? Why must you cause so many problems? You keep showing up to the party when no one wants you. You think you're so great for making so many people feel so bad. The truth of the matter is, peer pressure, you're nothing but a rude jerk, and it's time I put you in your place.

PEER PRESSURE

As you can probably tell, I have a lot of bones to pick with peer pressure. The first is its name—"peer pressure." If the people who are putting pressure on you are supposed to be your friends, they're not friends, they're goons.

So how do I deal with it when I'm "given the impression" that I have to try something or do something that makes me feel uncomfortable? I flash the hashtag, #thanksbutnothanks a.k.a. #sorrynotsorry.

Once you start giving in and going along with things, it snowballs. Bow to the pressure once and you'll be expected to bow deeper and deeper as time goes on. Before you know it, your nose will be on the ground and your self-respect will be in the gutter. So my advice is to stop it as soon as it starts. In other words, just say no. Because once you're known as the person who keeps your back straight and refuses to bend to the pressure, you'll be considered the strong one in the pack.

Handling Cliques

Cliques happen. One day you're cruising through school and everything's great and everyone's friends, and the next it feels like everyone has broken into little groups that include some people and exclude others. Now you might find yourself on the inside or the outside of a clique, but the reality is, just because you're on one side now doesn't mean you won't be on the other side at some point. So it's important to keep a few things in mind:

1. Regardless of your clique standing, give yourself the chance to meet all sorts of people. Being in a clique can be great because you feel entirely surrounded by friends. But if you only hang out with a set number of people, you'll be missing out on the awesomeness of others who don't happen to be in your group (for whatever reason). If you're not in a clique, try to meet people in your classes or in the activities you do, and you'll probably soon find that you have all sorts of great friends in many different groups.

2. Remember who you are and don't let group mentality change you. Just because everyone's doing the same thing doesn't mean you have to. Be you!

Read more about this in Chapter 9!

3. Don't be afraid to speak up and have your own opinion. Sometimes it's hard to tell people you disagree with them. But if they're your real friends, they'll want to know what you really think and have to say because they respect you.

Speak up!

Be you!

4. Respect yourself! Your friends do—don't you think you should trust in yourself, too?

5. Respect your friends. Showing mutual admiration is one of the best parts of being friends, so don't forget to be positive forces in each other's lives, and don't be afraid to let your friends know when they're doing great things (or talk to them when they're doing things that might be hurtful). When some of the kids at school were making Farkle feel bad for being different and not fitting in with the crowd, Riley, Maya, and Lucas showed him that they loved and respected him for exactly those reasons: he was Farkle, and he was awesome!

—Cory and Topanga

Don't get any ideas, Farkle.

School Dances Can Be Fun

Whenever I hear a school dance being announced, it's one of the best and worst days of my life. There is so much to look forward to, and so much to fear. Fortunately, most of you won't have to deal with the fact that your parents are also going to be chaperones at said dance. But having written the pro and con list on dances many, many times myself, I can tell you that the pros outnumber the cons by A LOT.

I'm not going to waste your time telling you about my worries when it comes to school dances, because there should only be positive ideas in your head. So let me tell you about why I think these dances are so much fun.

1. You get to dance! Your feet, legs, hips, arms, hands, neck, and head are free to do as they wish. They can move, shake, and shimmy in any direction they choose. When do you ever get to be so free at school?

2. You get to show off your moves! During the regular school day, the only way you get to show those off is in how you raise your hand in class or climb a rope in gym. You and I both know you've been practicing those dance steps in front of a mirror at home—the school dance is where you'll finally get the audience you deserve.

3. Hello, funky fresh outfit! This isn't a requirement, of course, but parents have been known to be very sympathetic to the "MUST GO SHOPPING BEFORE THE SCHOOL DANCE!" cry. So look at this as an opportunity to buy yourself something shiny and new. (Note: it totally doesn't need to be shiny!)

4. This is a great chance to talk to the cute person you've been crushing on. Look, I know from personal experience you're going to be nervous. But chances are, that person's going to be a little nervous, too. School dances bring out the nerves in EVERYONE. That's why if you can bring yourself to break the ice, putting your crush at ease through some casual conversation, you'll probably be on the dance floor together later in the night, moving and grooving!

See? I told you school dances could be fun!

SPRING DANCE

SATURDAY J.Q.A. AUDITORIUM

Being ~~Okay~~ amazing at Parties

Remember the days when you didn't have to think about anything before going to a party? Maybe you spent a minute or two wondering what present to get the birthday girl or boy. Guess what? Those "no-brainer" days are over. That's because now you spend more time thinking about the party before you go than the amount of time you'll actually be there.

Middle school parties can be tricky. That's because you can't always guess what you'll be walking into when you walk through that glittering party door. True story: Riley's first middle school party was NOT AT ALL what she was expecting. She had no idea who was on the guest list because, though in elementary school people had the "invite the whole class"-type gatherings, in middle school that's no longer the case.

Here's the good news: you're invited. That means people like you. So take a moment to bask in your own glow.

Okay, let's bring ourselves back to Earth.

Good, because we need to chat about how you're going to handle yourself at the party itself!

Let's start with a Fashion 411! What are you going to wear? Especially if you're new on the party circuit, I always think it's better to go casual (clean and simple) than aggressively trendy. Try to go for something in between fashion mag model and you on a regular school day—or like you're picking out clothes to wear for picture day. You want to dress to impress! And don't forget comfort!

Next, how should you act? Here, too, go casual. I always aim to be myself and not try too hard. You don't need to be the first person who volunteers to smack the piñata, and you don't need to attempt the splashiest cannonball at a pool party. But, yes, hit the dance floor, be social, and chat with other party people.

Speaking of: chat with different people and see who you can meet. Try to stay off your phone, too. Texting or scrolling through apps the whole time is not cute.

But be sure to take a ton of selfies!

And remember, everyone who goes to these things feels at least a little nervous. So be a good guest and help others feel good about being there, too.

How to Do the "Party-Girl Walk"

Maya has informed me that the "party-girl walk" isn't my strongest move. She also said it's probably better if I don't teach it to you here. So instead, I'm thinking you might want to make one up for yourself. Either that or use this time to practice your dazzling dance moves!

Yeah, Maya's totally right. Let's just stick to practicing some dance moves.

What Kind of Partygoer Are _YOU_?

1. What party outfit do you wear?

   a. Something trendy, cute, and comfy!
   b. I'll know when my bestie gets here.
   c. The most AWESOME outfit EVER!

2. At a party, you talk to:

   a. a handful of people.
   b. only my bestie.
   c. anyone and everyone.

3. The best part of the party is:

   a. enjoying all the drama from a distance.
   b. recapping events with my bestie after the party.
   c. hanging out or dancing with The Crush.

Score:

Mostly As: You are a people watcher! You enjoy keeping it low-key, mingling, and moving around the room. You hang with friends and go with the flow.

Mostly Bs: You're a bestie clinger. You're someone who can have fun just hanging out with your best friend. You two can have fun wherever you are.

Mostly Cs: You're the star of the party! You're the spirit of the room, and you come alive on a dance floor—especially with your fan club cheering you on.

Sleepover Activities

If you want to throw or attend a great sleepover, here are some ideas for you and your fab crew:

Have a spa night. Try avocado masks and manicures!

Prepare a yummy snack. Enjoy some chocolate fondue and fruit or create your own flavored popcorn.

Make friendship bracelets. Use accessories you no longer wear.

Give each other makeovers. Do crazy hair and makeup and post before-and-after videos online. Try finding how-to videos online first for inspiration.

Make a music video for your favorite song. Dare to post it?

Play Truth or Dare!

Create a scavenger hunt for your guests. Break up into teams and have prizes for the team who finds the most stuff!

Scavenger Hunt
- two-dollar bill
- blue straw
- sugar packet
- silver button
- a violet

New York City
Field Trip

We don't always get invited to parties. And for most of the ones we fail to receive invites to, it's completely fine with us. Maybe the host isn't a good friend, or they could only invite a small number of people, or whatever. We get it. But occasionally, when we don't get invited somewhere, it kind of stings.

So because it has happened to us, we've tried to come up with ways to lessen the pain. What we've realized is that planning an adventure for the party period in question helps hugely. Since we live in New York, we like to bop around the city and check out some of the amazing sights by night. Here are a few of our favorites:

Museum of Modern Art

The Empire State Building

Grand Central Terminal

The Brooklyn Bridge

Coney Island

Top Secret

You weren't invited to a party. So you decide to go on a field trip with a friend instead. Even better! Come up with your own list of places where you can go and what you'd like to do there.

Where did you go? What did you do?
Write about your own field trip below!

Top Secret 2.0 1.0

Sometimes having a friend over for a sleepover is just as cool as a field trip. Did any of our sleepover activities sound like fun? Do you have any of your own? Write about what you like to do on a night in.

Z
Z
Z
Z

Chapter 8

Big World, Bigger Problems!

True Beauty Secrets

You've probably noticed some people hit major growth spurts in middle school. I just so happen to be one of those tall-ish people! Maya's still waiting for her big spurt, but it should happen aaaany day now. . . . (Don't you worry, Maya!) As a bigger person, you're going to take up more space, and because there's more of you, it's even more important to keep your body in good shape. We consider "good shape" to mean being clean and healthy. So let's start with the head and work our way down!

Hair: Whether you like to wear it long, short, spiked, or gelled, whether you want to change its color or play with your hair's texture, I say go for it! I happen to think it's fun to experiment with different hairstyles, because even if you do mess it up, no biggie, hair grows back. The only hair "do," therefore, is "keep that hairdo clean." (PS: From what I've heard, the number of times you need to shampoo and condition your hair in a week depends on its specific texture, so also double-check with a stylist or on the blogs to learn what's best for your particular hair type.)

<u>Face:</u> I hate to be the bearer of bad news, but over the next few years, your skin is going to betray you. Pimples WILL appear. They will strike you in expected and unexpected places. Each zit that crops up will make you curse the universe. I've learned that there are options:

1. Acne cream. You can buy it almost anywhere, and it does a great job drying out those oil slicks and reducing their size.

2. Dermatologists. These doctors deal with "problem" skin all the time and have some killer medications that fight fire with fire.

3. Face wash. Wash your face every night before bed. It will help keep pimples away before they form.

4. Good diet. Avoiding sugary, greasy foods helps, at least for me. Every time I eat them, my face breaks out. But everyone's skin is different, so know the skin you're in and act accordingly.

<u>Core:</u> Water, lather, scrub, repeat. Yep, that should take care of it!

<u>Claws:</u> You have over a dozen nails. You can paint 'em, leave them au naturel, wear them long, or cut them short. But however you want them to look, just remember that dirty = disgusting. You'll be in good shape as long as you make sure they stay ick-free, because from what I've seen, the last thing anyone wants to hold is a grubby, nasty hand with dirt under some yellow, jagged nails.

Conquering GYM CLASS

I won't lie to you. I hate gym class. When I think of a place I want to send my enemies, gym comes to mind. I know its purpose is to make us do physical activity, and that part of the mission seems like a decent enough idea. But I'd rather clean a public restroom with my toothbrush. So in trying to find a way to make gym somewhat bearable, I came up with ideas that I'll share, because I feel your pain:

1. If the activity you're forced to do requires a ball and a racket, do yourself a favor and picture your least favorite teacher's head on the ball. Then approach it and strike it with all of your might. Too evil? Scratch that.

2. If the fitness test is having to run some crazy distance, don't think of it as running a useless mile for gym. Think of it as preparing for your escape from the coming zombie apocalypse! Too scary? So let's nix that one, too.

3. I hate to admit it, but I guess the best thing to do is to be positive and power through it. When else are you going to get energized but in gym class? And who knows— maybe you'll even impress The Crush with a killer volleyball move.

I Want to Paint My Face!

You know what I've never understood? The makeup trend known as "the natural look." I mean, what's the point? If I'm going to wear makeup, I want everyone to know I'm wearing makeup!

My mom and dad don't want me to wear any makeup at all. They tell me my face is beautiful just the way it is, and that's nice of them to say. Then again, they're my parents and they LITERALLY made me look this way, so they're actually just complimenting themselves. A big reason my parents don't want me to wear makeup is because they think it'll make me look older.

Hello? That's one of the reasons why I want to wear it!

A bigger reason my parents gave me was that they were worried that wearing makeup would lower my self-esteem.

My parents thought I would feel like I needed to look like someone else if I wore makeup. But I thanked them for their concern and told them that even if I'm insecure sometimes (see page 129), I know self-confidence is really what makes you look best. When you believe in yourself, it really shines through, and that's the first gloss you should always apply. As it turned out, that was something we could all agree on.

Be Proud of How You Look

Do you look in the mirror and shudder at the sight of yourself? If that's the case, you need two cents of advice from Mama Maya. I'll start out by saying that you were born in the skin you're in, so there's really no use not liking how you look. You look like you, which is cool.

If you're not pleased with how you look, your mind and your body should really give up on their civil war and just make peace already. There. That's more like it. You see, whatever your culture is, your genetics, your background, you are one unique-looking person. Own that. Rock it out. I know feeling great about yourself isn't some kind of switch you can just turn on if it's been off. But if you remind yourself how great you are, that shining soul of yours will illuminate your physical self. And people will notice your beauty. As cheesy as it sounds, beauty really does come from within.

There is a lot of pressure from society and media to look a certain way. But, honey, you look great in the skin you're in, just as you are. So take a moment to soak that up.

Be proud of how you look, because your physical self is representing that beautiful soul of yours! And if you happen to already be proud of how you look, you're doing great. Keep it up!

Beauty's Skin-Deep

Regardless of what you look like, we want to emphasize how important it is to FEEL GOOD. That's why we wanted to do this brief musical interlude to remind you that you can be the most symmetrical fashion model in town, but if you're mean or rude or unkind or ignorant, you ain't cute.

When you're not a good person, as soon as you open your mouth or roll your eyes at someone (a mean-girl signature move), ugliness seeps out. And it covers you like cheap, bad-smelling perfume. So it doesn't matter how physically "perfect" you are; if you have a cruel streak, you're a train wreck.

On the other hand—the BETTER hand— regardless of what you look like on the outside, if you have a great heart, warm personality, and kindness, those are the things people will remember about you. Being a sweetie is like getting spray-tanned with glitter; you shine. And no matter the size or shape of your least favorite trait, the shine is what people see first, because true beauty glows from the inside out!

Wear Your Flaws

We all know what a "typically pretty" person looks like. They have a "nice" and "standard" appearance. But when someone has a feature that stands out—maybe it's a crooked nose, a mole, a scar, a gap between the teeth, a limp, or wide-set eyes—the person instantly becomes "unusual." Guess what! When you're unusual, it makes you unique. And when you're unique, you're unforgettable. Sure, I understand why people just want to blend into the crowd sometimes. But having something that makes you stand out in that crowd is better. *always!*

I know what you're thinking: Maya, why? Why? Why? Why would I want a "strange" feature? And why would I want to embrace that feature?

Because I want you to think of it this way: vanilla is fine and dandy, but who chooses plain old vanilla when they could have mint chip, chocolate-chip cookie dough, or rocky road fudge swirl instead? It's the unique flavors that are so much more delicious.

It's your unique traits that make you more appealing, too!

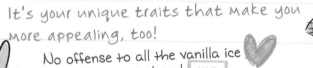

No offense to all the vanilla ice cream fans out there!

Top Secret

What makes you feel good without fail?

Write down a few things that make you feel crummy. Then write down ways to handle them so you feel good!

Hygiene Advice

I know I'm going to sound like a mom when I say this, but sometimes having someone else's mom say it lets you hear it in a way you never would if _your_ mom told you. And I _know_ you already know these things, but when it comes to hygiene, it never hurts to restate the obvious. So here are the golden rules, otherwise known as the things you should be doing to take care of yourself every day:

1. Brush your teeth (do this one 2x/day) & floss.

2. Take a shower.

3. Use ear swabs.

4. Wear deodorant.

5. Brush your hair (unless it's curly, then you're excused).

6. Change your clothes and/or wash your clothes.

7. Underwear. Wear it. Then change it.

8. Keep your nails clean.

9. Wash your hands.

10. Wash your face.

11. Get enough sleep.

12. Repeat.

Topanga

Chapter 9

Accept Me for ME, World!
Be Okay Just Being Yourself

Know what I like best about Halloween? The fact that it only comes once a year. Don't get me wrong. I love coming up with a costume, rocking the new look, and facing my fears (okay, maybe I don't LOVE facing my fears). But at the end of the night, once I've come back from the parties and trick-or-treating, what I like most is getting to scrub off all the makeup, pack the costume away, and return to just being me.

Yeah, it's fun pretending you're someone else every once in a while. That's what fantasy is all about. But I think it's even cooler when you're psyched to dress up as YOU each day. When you know who you are—meaning you know what you love, hate, and want—it's like you have a superpower. That's because you're not looking for other people to set the example for you. You decide what looks, feels, and sounds good, and it's not up to anyone else.

YOU own your decisions! Now THAT'S powerful.

133

Being Unique Is Incredible

Do you know or have you ever known someone you really admired? I'm talking about having feelings of deep and profound awe for someone. They might be a little older than you or maybe they're in your class, and you think they're cooler than cool. Everything this person does is beyond amazing—whether they're a student government leader, a fantastic musician, or just know how to fry a mean egg. They're unique, a one and only, and that's part of the reason why you admire them.

I know it's hard to believe, but you, too, have unique qualities that make you who you are—and they're exactly what people love about you. That's why you should never let anyone convince you to give up doing the things you enjoy or being quirky in the way that you are just so you can fit in. Just like that person you look up to, you are super special.

Believe in Yourself

When it comes time for class elections, someone always asks the candidates if they're going to vote for themselves. I think how the candidates answer says a lot about them. My dad always told me that if I run for something, I should definitely vote for myself. He said, "Riley, if you don't believe that you can do a great job then you shouldn't be running for office in the first place." He said strong people have faith in themselves, and that was one of the lessons he learned from his teacher and mentor, Mr. Feeny. So even though I don't run for elections every day, I think it's a great piece of advice.

By now, you know me: I can feel majorly insecure about things. I worry about failing or embarrassing myself. Or both! But I know the reality is if I believe in myself more, nothing will stop me. And even if I do fail, if I have the confidence to try again, chances are I'll do better the second time around.

So this is one of those things I think we should work on: let's spend more time dreaming about what we want to accomplish. The world is in desperate need of dreamers and do-gooders, and if you can lead the way, we'll all be much better off.

Top Secret

DREAM BIG! Write down a list of ALL the things you want to accomplish . . .

TODAY:

THIS WEEK:

THIS MONTH:

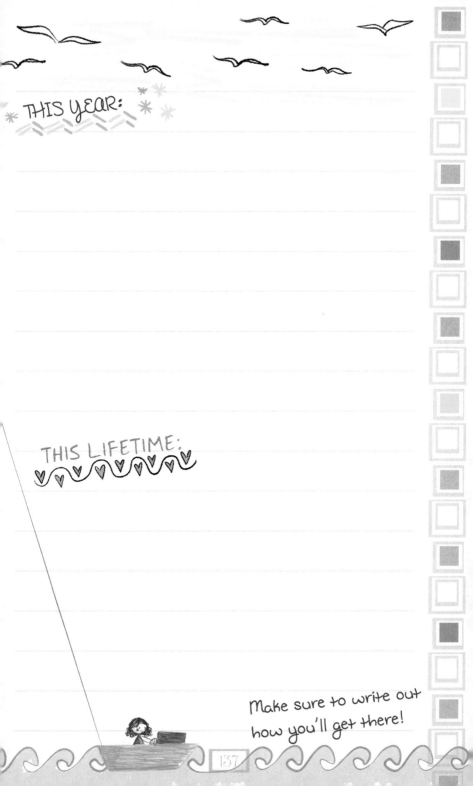

THIS YEAR:

THIS LIFETIME:

Make sure to write out how you'll get there!

Positive Influences and Dreaming BIG

Whether your idol is Beyoncé, Sally Ride, Oprah, your teacher, or your parents, it's nice to have someone to look up to. It's cool to see how that someone you respect handles the challenges that life throws at them. Gammy Hart told me that even though successful people seem to have it all figured out, at one point they were just confused middle schoolers, too. As hard as it may be to believe, that means they somehow got to where they are today after being in exactly the same position you're in now. Amazing, isn't it?

So the question is, how did your idol do it? How did they get to the top? Unfortunately, Beyoncé and I aren't as close as I'd like us to be, so I only know what I've read in magazines. But from all the interviews I've seen, the answers are hard work and making mistakes. The hard work thing makes sense, because you don't just arrive at the top by accident, and for most people it isn't a stroke of luck, either. So chances are, if this is someone you genuinely respect, he or she has worked hard to earn that respect. So take note!

Any successful person has also made a ton of mistakes. From the outside that usually isn't noticeable. But I bet you if you ask the person what turned them into who they are, they'll tell you it was learning from their follies.

I make mistakes all the time. But I think it's how a person reacts to the mess-ups that separates the winners from the losers. If you give up and say the thing is too hard after you've botched something, you'll never succeed. That's pretty much the only thing you can count on. But if you keep trying (and trying), you may wind up the next president, CEO, or winner of an EGOT—the Emmy, Grammy, Oscar, and Tony! That's why I think it's important to have positive role models to look up to. Because these people not only show you what's possible to achieve if you work hard (and if you've seen Beyoncé's show, you know what a hard worker she is), but they also show you how to bounce back from setbacks. As Mr. Matthews says, "A setback is a setup for a comeback."

So don't be afraid to aim high with your own goals and take calculated risks, because you just never know what you'll achieve if you go for it!

Never give up!!

Top Secret ??

Who is someone you really respect?
Write down a list of all their good qualities!

Do you have any of these qualities? Which ones? Which ones would you like to have? Write it out!

Happy-Dance Away!

When Topanga and I were your age, we were pretty sure we had life all figured out. We'd been hanging around planet Earth for more than a decade, so we were confident that we knew how to get along in the world. That's why it came as such a shock to us when we met some new kids at the beach one summer and they were totally mean to us! Remember, Topanga?

Oh, yeah! They were awful. They made fun of the way you talked, the Hawaiian-print swim trunks you wore, and they even mocked the little victory dance you did whenever you managed to catch the Frisbee.

What did they make fun of you about?

That I was standing next to you.

Oh, right. Well, anyway, we saw these kids every day that summer, and I realized that if I just started wearing the same kind of trunks they did, talked like they did, and stopped doing my happy dance, I could fit in with them much better.

But you didn't do that, did you?

No, I did not.

And why not, my love?

Well, first of all, I know how much you love my happy dance.

Very true. Watching you prance around like that never fails to put a smile on my face!

Right . . . Anyway, the other reason I decided not to change up my style was because I remembered the wise words my teacher and mentor, Mr. Feeny, gave me earlier that year. He said, "If you let people's perception of you dictate your behavior, you'll never grow as a person."

Mr. Feeny was always a wise, wise man! And his point is as true today as it was back when we were your age: being yourself is awesome, and if that's different from everyone else, not only is that okay, it's <u>cool</u>.

So if someone's not going to accept you for the unique person and happy-dancer you are, it is very much their loss!

—Cory
and Topanga

How Would Your Friend Describe You?

Kid, if what I hear in the teachers' lounge is true, you're extraordinary. Now I could tell you all of the amazing qualities your teachers have mentioned to me about you, but I'd love to hear what one of your friends thinks are your best traits. So why don't you hand this book over to a friend and tell them to take a crack at writing down everything they like about you.

-Cory

FROM THE DESK OF CORY MATTHEWS

My friend is ... Jahiyah.B

I'll never forget the time my friend . . .

I love my friend because . . .

I want my friend to know . . .

Start Your Day with Confidence! ♥♥

- ☐ Teeth brushed
- ☐ Showered and dressed
- ☐ Breakfast consumed
- ☐ Backpack filled with books and homework
- ☐ Out door in time to catch ride to school
- ☐ Hellos said to friends
- ☐ Unneeded stuff stashed in locker
- ☐ Smiles given to teachers
- ☐ Tushy in chair before bell rings

Chapter 10

The Future of the World . . . Is YOU! What's Next, World?

Know your strengths. I don't want to brag, but I am really, really, REALLY good at academia. I also happen to be an excellent bed-maker. Maya is an _amazing_ singer. She's also awesome at art (which we all know).

Thanks, Riles!

But I don't want you to think that just because Maya and I are good at some things that we're good at EVERYTHING. In fact, here's a list of things I stink at:

1. Anything athletic
2. Blowing bubbles
3. Not spilling on myself when I bite into a burrito
4. Video games
5. Lying
6. Cooking
7. Sitting still on long car rides
8. Not freaking out

(This list is actually a lot longer than I thought. . . .)
My point is that EVERYBODY has weaknesses. And despite the fact that everyone is going to have things that they can't do well (no matter how hard they try), we all have things we can do amazingly.

So instead of being worried about what you aren't great at or being insecure about what you think of as your weaknesses, think about all your strengths and your "weaknesses" will wind up fading into the background! Once you do that, the future is yours for the taking!

Embrace Your History and Control Your DESTINY

Mr. Matthews is always trying to get me to study history. Since he's a history teacher, I can't really hold it against him. But until this year, I have to admit I didn't really see the point. History was in the past, and my feeling was "what's done is done." I was much more interested in what was going to happen in the future (in MY future). But Mr. Matthews kept saying things like, "If we don't learn our history, we'll be doomed to repeat it!" which sounded a little desperate to me, you know?

But he followed up with examples of how people kept making the same mistakes, and he said if they'd actually just thought about the decision their ancestors made, they could have saved themselves time, money, and heartache. As a person who doesn't have a lot of time, even less money, and is not cruising for a bruising in the heart department, I started thinking about what he said. It also helped that he then gave us an assignment to research ou great-grandparents to show us our "living history."

What I learned was that if there was something in the past that didn't turn out the way I liked—for instance how my great-grandmother, May Clutterbucket, gave up on her dream—I didn't have to repeat her mistake. Mr. Matthews taught me that "history isn't destiny." Life's about choosing your own fate. Once you know one path, you can pick another and wind up in a better place. X•X•X•X•X•X•X•X•X

Remember that all the stuff that's happened—the good, the bad, and the ugly—has been what's made you YOU. My family has gone through some hard times. I found that even when I was in the roughest spots, I went down creative (and not destructive) paths, which is good because that's what'll lead you to a promising new future. I discovered new things about myself, like that I'm an artist. And that I'm strong—way stronger than I assumed. That's when I understood my own history was something that I should respect. My history, like yours, is what's made me, ME, and you, YOU. X•X•X•X

So be proud of your past and the things that helped make you the person you are today. You're not going to shrink back and follow in anyone's footsteps that aren't right for you. You decide the course of your life, because don't you want to be the one driving that powerful train for yourself?

Top Secret

Family tree! Do your best to draw your family tree as far back as you can. Feel free to list traditions!

What are some of your family members' life stories? Are there paths you'd like to follow? How about new paths you'd like to create?

How Will You Affect YOUR World?

If you couldn't already tell, we're nearing the end of our book. Maya and I are almost out of advice on the topic of "You in Middle School." And by this point, we're feeling fairly confident that you've been introduced to this brave new world. So now that you've gotten this far, there's a big old point we'd like for you to ponder:

How will you affect YOUR world?

Just like my dad told me when I started middle school, "It's YOUR world now." You can choose to be whoever you want. You can create your own style. You can set goals for yourself. You can (and should!) figure out what you love to spend your time doing and find ways to do it more often. The bottom line is that you have the potential to make changes in yourself and your world. In history we learned about Dr. Martin Luther King Jr., and when he gave his famous "I Have a Dream" speech at the march on Washington, he told the large group of protesters that they should expect more. He inspired them to dream about a better future.

We can all help make the future better for ourselves and for those around us. Like Dr. King, we just need to have the dream!

Certificate of AWESOMENESS

The Bearer of This Document Will Take On the World by Feeling Great About Themselves, Staying Positive, and Always Following Their Dreams.

(sign here)

Riley and Maya

Middle Schoolers

©Disney

My Life, My World!
Let Me Be ME!

"Let me be me!" I've said that to my parents so many times it's practically my ringtone. But ever since I got to middle school, getting to express myself and show the world who I am has been super important to me. Sure, who "ME" is might change on a daily basis. One day I'm into Top 40 music, the next I only want to hear electronic dance music. One day I want to be a cheerleader, the next the Quizbowl captain.

But whoever I am today or am hoping to become tomorrow, there's one thing that's going to stay true: I'm always going to try to be a good friend and daughter—and sister, too, I guess. Even though my family might not always agree with my choice of clothes or might nag me to do things I don't want to do, and even though our opinions about lots of stuff may differ, I know that they have my back. They want the best for me. And even though my being in middle school seems to put our relationship to the test at times, I know we'll all get through it together.

As for my good friends, since they feel like family to me, the same thing holds true. If I ever need them, they're here for me, and if they need anything, they can be 100 percent sure that they can count on me.

Now It's <u>YOUR</u> Turn

Congratulations! Now that you've also arrived here at the "point of no return," a.k.a. middle school, your life really begins! Yeah, you were somebody before. But now people are going to take you more seriously, and the choices you make are going to matter.

It's kinda cool and kinda scary, right?

The good news is you're up for the challenge. If you just stay true to yourself, follow your heart, and try your best through all the stuff that middle school throws at you, you'll be headed toward your happy ending!

Make Your World YOURS

Guess what? At this point we think we've told you everything we've learned about life and middle school so far. So as someone very wise once said, "I've already met the world. It's your turn." *and related to Riley* We hope some of the stories we've told and the things we've figured out will help make things a little easier for you.

We know the next few years are going to be fun, challenging, exciting, terrifying, and full of love stories, drama, comedy, and adventure. As a great old song goes, "now it's time to say good-bye . . ." Just know we're always with you and cheering you on!

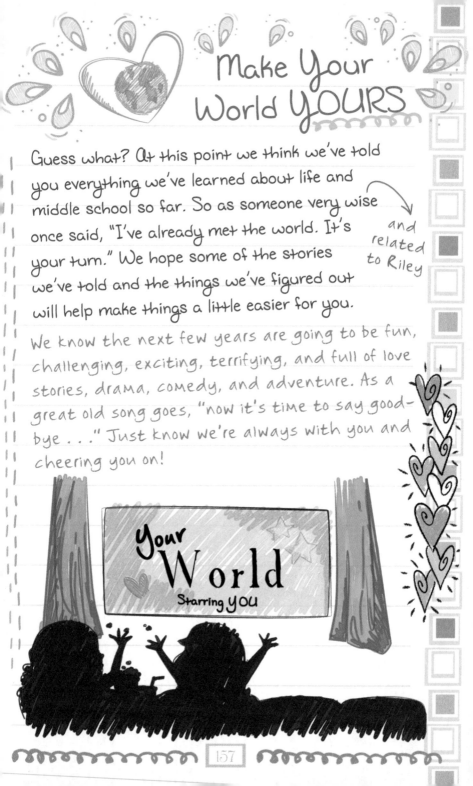

Your World
Starring YOU

Top Secret

Write about how you're going to make your middle school years great! We know you will!

Is there anything you're nervous about? Write down your fears about middle school and then look at the letters. Rearrange the letters from your fears and turn them into positive words or goals for your middle school experience!

Now that's more like it!

NICE JOB!

Fears:

Positives:

We really hope our tips and tricks help you <u>OWN</u> middle school. Enjoy it! And if the going gets tough, just remember it's temporary! And you'll graduate middle school like a beautiful butterfly, ready to take flight and share your colors with the world.

Keep it real!

Stay positive!

Stand up for what you believe in.

Follow your heart.

Eat cake.

Keep it weird!

Be a good friend.

Riley and Maya's Fortune Teller

Find out what _YOUR_ world has in store for YOU!

How to make your Fortune Teller:

1. Cut on the solid lines.

2. Fold your square in half, then in half again. Now unfold it!

3. Putting the fortunes facedown, fold each corner point into the center.

4. Now flip it over (flap side down). Fold those corner points into the center.

5. Fold in half to crease it, then unfold. Next fold in half the other way.

6. Stick your thumbs and first two fingers into the pockets. Push all the pockets to the center, and you're ready to play!

How to play:

1. Pick one of the four words.

2. Open and close the Fortune Teller for each letter of the word.

3. Pick one of the numbers inside the Fortune Teller.

4. Open and close the Fortune Teller that many times.

5. Do steps 3 and 4 one more time.

6. Choose one of the numbers and open the flap to reveal the fortune beneath it!